"You'll never be happy with just one man...

"If I were you, I'd get rid of them all, Andrea.
Just disappear for a while and start all over again.
You've caused one murder and maybe another is
festering right now. You can't toy with people's
emotions and expect them to come up with flowers—
unless they're lilies. And honey, baby, the way things
are going, those lilies might be for you."

Andrea Lockridge was as beautiful
as she was insatiable. At least
six men found her an unbreakable
habit. She had planned to marry
a millionaire, but he was murdered
before he could get to the altar.
Now she was making new plans to
marry. But the question was,
would Andrea or her latest love
be the next to die?

These Lonely, These Dead

Robert Colby

PROLOGUE BOOKS

F + W Media, Inc.

Published in electronic format by
PROLOGUE BOOKS
an imprint of F+W Media, Inc.
10151 Carver Road
Blue Ash, Ohio 45242
www.prologuebooks.com

eISBN 10: 1-4405-3921-9
eISBN 13: 978-1-4405-3921-3
POD ISBN 10: 1-4405-5802-7
POD ISBN 13: 978-1-4405-5802-3

This is a work of fiction. Names, characters, corporations, institutions, organizations, events, or locales in this novel are either the product of the author's imagination or, if real, used fictitiously. The resemblance of any character to actual persons (living or dead) is entirely coincidental.

This work has been previously published in print format by:
Pyramid Books, New York, NY.

The Murderer

IN THE DARKNESS I held my wrist close to my face and pulled hard on the cigarette until it glowed brightly and I could see the dial of my watch. It was twenty minutes past two A.M.

I flipped the butt out the convertible. It tumbled in a high arc and fell to the street with a small shower of sparks. Bending, I groped around the floorboards until my hand touched the metal coolness of the long barrel. For the third time in the past hour I laid the high-powered .30-06 rifle across my knees and peered ahead out of the foggy darkness of the side street into the bright, misty glow of the street lamp in front of the apartment building a hundred yards beyond.

The building was three stories, a low, wood frame structure painted pale green with white trim. It was shaped like a boomerang, the open ends fronting the street and enclosing a wide sweep of neatly manicured lawn. Tall palm trees nudged the building and rose above it. Flowers, mostly red geraniums, followed the interior edge of the lawn.

Altogether there was the rambling, informal effect of an oversized cottage. It was a type of apartment house you seldom see anywhere but in California or Florida. The lawn was split at the center by a straight flagstone walk which had three steps at the entrance. Above the steps where the walk began, two wrought iron lamps, like rustic sentries, added to the illumination from the street light.

But where I sat behind the wheel of the open convertible, the darkness was total.

There was the threat of rain in the air. You could smell it. The sky was overcast and without moon or stars. Fog had crept in from the Santa Monica coast line only a few blocks away, so that even on lighted thoroughfares, you couldn't see farther than the beginning of the next block.

I remember how it was when I wound up the hill from the ocean highway and swung over to Wilshire where it begins—or ends—at the Miramar Hotel. The usual blaze of rainbow gaudy neon that glowed from miles of restaurants, drive-ins, movies and bars, had a sad, washed-out look, as though somehow the pleasures they advertised had paled and even this gloomy mention of them was embarrassing.

It was eerie, too. Like the dim blue neon words that cling to the faces of those streamlined funeral parlors you see on almost every other block in Los Angeles. Never bright or cheerful. Always dim, always blue. As though apologizing with gloomy unctuousness for death. It occurred to me that a blaze of red might be amusing for these parlors. Certainly more fitting. Pale blue is such a ghastly excuse for death.

Anyway, it was a night I was waiting for. I needed the overcast sky. I planned for it. But the fog was a bonus. It followed a week of brilliant April nights during which I was chained to inaction like a snarling dog with rabies. And of course the whole dirty thing was going on just the same. Every night. It didn't wait for me.

I saw a light on in that known square of window on the second floor left, about ten minutes to three. I knew then that he'd be down in a few minutes. For some twisted reason of female propriety, she never let him stay overnight. People talk, you know. They catch on. I did.

He came down a couple of minutes after three. Howard D. Overholtzer did. Isn't that a name! Howie, she called him. Jesus! You've got to have a lot of money to get away with a name like Howard D. Overholtzer. He did.

He was wearing that white shantung jacket, blue trousers, midnight blue I think he called them, and a

cute little red bow tie. God! They had been dancing
most of the evening at the Ambassador. Then they went
on to Mocambo's. I know. I followed them. At a very
discreet distance. I could have ended it then—when
they came home. But she was right on his arm. And
while I'm a hell of a good shot, there was always the
chance . . .

He came sauntering down the walk. Very pleased
with himself. He looked so neat, so shining; his black
hair parted in the middle and combed straight back
off his suave, clever little features, sun dark the year
round. Close up his eyes were ripe olive dark—and
narrow, which gave him a slightly Oriental look. He
was a big one, a little pudgy—but, oh sure, I'll admit,
damn good looking. If you like the type.

He was always so immaculate. Even now. You never
would think that she had so much as mussed his hair.
You never would think that he had just now crept out
of her bed, rumple-haired, a little damp-skinned, lipstick smeared grotesquely around the corners of his
fat mouth. (She always did wear too much lipstick,
I'll have to admit.)

He would pull on his shorts over the brown thighs
and brown-white buttocks. And then maybe he would
comb his hair very carefully as he sat in front of her
vanity mirror, fastidiously removing every trace of lipstick. Remember that mirror? How we used to tilt it
a little?

And then he would put on the rest of his clothes with
great attention to neatness and detail—as though he
were dressing for . . . for his own funeral. He was!

I thought about things like that as he came down the
walk. Not the other part. I shut off the writhing pictures of them together long before. I couldn't allow
those crawling, obscene images to destroy the needed
calm I had built so carefully.

I knelt on the leather seat and let the gun barrel rest
on the top rim of the windshield. It was good leverage.
The rifle butt was firm in the socket of my shoulder,
my finger was steady as it slipped under the trigger

guard and began to take up slack. I had cocked the gun when he came out the door.

He approached the two wrought iron lamps and the wisps of gray around him diminished. His chest was a perfect target in the cross-hairs of the telescopic sight. But I liked the look of his high, broad forehead and inched up to just below the greasy part in his hair. He wasn't going anywhere, even if the first shot missed. You don't recover from shock that quickly unless you're expecting that you might be shot down fresh out of a warm bed next to a warmer body. He wasn't. And I was crazy about the proud look of his forehead. Howard D. Overholtzer.

He came almost directly into the light. And then he turned away suddenly and walked back under her window. She was calling something, I imagine. He waited there and in a minute or two she joined him, Andrea "Andy" Lockridge did, wearing that tight red sweater and gray skirt. The way her breasts bounced when she walked, you could tell she had just thrown the outfit on, that she wasn't wearing a brassiere, if anything, underneath. Bitch!

Andy Lockridge is tall. She's built like an Amazon. A goddess of Amazons. She *is* a kind of goddess to me. She has marvelous red hair. Not that cheap bright red. More the color of umber. Subdued. But shiny. It hangs way down her back and makes a soft frame for her face, which is kind of heart-shaped. And full. Not a sharp feature anywhere, though she has high, rounded cheekbones. Her eyes are green like emeralds and have more sparkle. Though sometimes they're heavy-lidded and dreamy. I like her most then. But her mouth is the best. I've watched men when they first meet her. They go all gnat-eyed flitting from her mouth to her breasts and wondering where to light first.

She has a thirty-eight inch bust. I know what you're thinking. But she's twenty-four and it'll be years before she ever begins to sag. Anywhere. She's big but she doesn't own an ounce of fat. Her breasts, especially the way she holds herself—shoulders back, seem to precede her as she comes into a room, trumpeting her entrance. From there on down she tapers beautifully, like inverted parentheses. Only she's very long-waisted. And she has the longest legs I've ever seen. And the best. Absolutely the best. That's Andy Lockridge. To look at.

They came walking arm in arm to his ten-thousand-dollar Lincoln Continental. I figured that he had invited her for a drink at one of those after-hour places he always knew where to find. And that proved to be the case later. She had refused, then changed her mind. She was the restless, energetic kind that didn't like to sleep until the first light of day drained all the excitement out of the night.

My God, but that was an awful moment! I was more tense than I knew and I wasn't going to be able to wait any longer. I could feel the dam breaking away from that eternal patience, that week of terrible control. And they probably wouldn't be back till daylight. I had to chance it.

So when they came abreast of the lamps, I was ready. I was already squeezing the trigger when his big head lit up in the cross-hairs.

Oh my God, what a sound! It seemed to knock on every window. It seemed to accuse back at me from every building. He didn't clutch at his head or anything dramatic like that. If he made a sound, I didn't hear it. He acted as if someone had given him a shove, so hard it snapped his head back. He began to topple backwards. Unresistingly. Not the way people do when they're off balance, flailing the air. Of course he was already dead. The shot had jammed his right eye through the back of his head. But I didn't know that then. It was just luck.

Andrea was still holding onto his arm. But he was sagging back. His weight was too much for her. He was doing a back-bend. His chest had disappeared. His abdomen was pushed toward me. It gave me an idea. If you can get an idea at such a time. It was just a lightning flash of inspiration. I lowered my aim and

fired again, just above the apex of his legs. Into the
groin. It gave me a certain real satisfaction. Later. I
was in a frenzy then.

He was on the ground now, one leg extended, the
other cocked at the knee and canted strangely. She was
bending over him. When she straightened suddenly
and screaming, pressed the palms of her hands against
her temples, beautiful even then, I knew it was over.
He was dead. Howard Donald Overholtzer. Just a
name.

I began to be afraid then. I could feel the first edge
of panic. But as I backed the convertible, lights out, to
the next cross street, there was underneath the fear,
this elation. He was dead. And she had seen it. She had
stared into the bloody ooze that was his face.

I put the top up as I drove slowly parallel to Wilshire.
I closed the windows. I switched on the lights. I remembered not to hurry. I turned left on Ocean Avenue
and right at the entrance to Santa Monica Pier. I slid
down the ramp and rumbled over the dock—all the
way to the end.

It was dark. There wasn't a light showing anywhere.
At this hour, the water taxi pilot would be asleep on
his cot in the cubicle a flight below. I parked by the
railing and cut the lights. I got out and looked around
carefully. There was no one. I went back and got the
rifle and an oily rag. I wiped it carefully. Water might
erase and it might not. I didn't know.

I went to the rail farthest from the pilot's cubicle. I
leaned over with the rifle. I held it vertically, barrel
down. I let it go. I couldn't see it, but it made a small
splash, a minimum sound. I got back in the car and
lighted a cigarette. I listened. It had taken them a long
time. But finally I heard the siren—far in the distance.
Then another. And later, still a third. But after awhile,
it was quiet and I began to relax.

I didn't spend any time thinking about Overholtzer.
I forgot him right away. But she crept back into my
consciousness almost immediately. I remembered the
way her breasts thrust against the red sweater, the

way they bounced when she came out of the apartment house. And more than any time in my life, I wanted her. The need was unbearable. Greater than my fear.

I knew that I wasn't going to have her for—what? Maybe a week? Two weeks at the most. She would recover fast. Because she had her own needs—more driving and varied than mine. There was nothing now to hold her by a thin thread out of circulation. Overholtzer was going to marry her. But he was dead. Now she would be as unconfined as before. And as willing. I would wait.

I settled back in the seat and fell into a hazy night dream, eyes open. It was some vague time in the future. We were in Andrea's apartment. I sat next to her on the couch. A single light glowed from a table lamp. Her head rested on my shoulder. She was sobbing. I stroked her head. I consoled her, said all the right things. After awhile she stopped crying and I kissed her. All her pentup emotion had to go somewhere. She poured it in that kiss. And the hand that had killed her lover, pulled up slowly on the red sweater. After that it was easy.

I spent the next hour imagining it. Then I started the motor and slowly, being very careful not to infringe on the smallest traffic regulation, I drove home.

Dawn was just breaking as I climbed into bed. The fog had vanished. The sun promised to be bright and warm. It was going to be a beautiful day.

Andrea Lockridge

HOWIE OVERHOLTZER will be calling for me any minute now. He says we're going to the Coconut Grove over at the Ambassador. Exciting! I like Freddy Martin's music. And it's Saturday night. They'll have a good floor show. But, oh Lord, those crowds! Well . . .

Hope I look all right. This strapless is a little bold, maybe. If they took off another couple of inches I'd pop right out at the top. Wouldn't that be something! There'd be more than me popping. Every eye in the room would pop, too. In a way, I'd like that. Anyway, I simply adore this green satin. It matches my eyes.

Think I'll make myself a martini. I don't like to drink alone. I don't like to do anything alone. Ha! But I'm very excited tonight. And a little nervous. Where did I put that shaker? Oh, here! They say you should just stir a martini. Well . . .

I just hope everything goes well. Eight more days and we'll be married. Hardly out of college and a mi' lionaire. Or is it millionairess? What's the difference? Of course, it's his money. But after—isn't it mine, too? Even if we didn't get along, or if I just got tired of him, he'd have to give me half under California law. That wonderful community property thing.

But if it doesn't happen. If we don't get married— I'm nothing. Just nothing. Of course, I have the ring. Look at it. Just look at it! If you didn't know it was real, you wouldn't believe it. I'll bet it cost him twenty-five—no, maybe fifty thousand. Have it appraised sometime. But what's the ring if the marriage doesn't come off? He might even take it back. Wonder if I'm handling him right? Wonder if I should be sleeping with him every night? He could get tired of it. Huh! Not him. He's insatiable. But then, so am I.

12

Mmmmm. This is good. I don't make such a bad martini. Good Lord! Hope I don't become a dipso on top of everything else. But there's a cure for that. Wonder if there's a cure for sex? Huh! There couldn't be. And even if there was, I wouldn't want to take it.

Howie isn't bad that way, you know? He's kind of artless. But he makes up for it with unlimited animal energy. Still—he would wear thin after awhile. He's not one of the ones that makes you want to scream for more. Like Jeff. Or Doug Coleman. Doug! I haven't seen him in ages. Well, a week or so. Wonder what he's up to now? Haven't seen Jeff either. Or Mark Bristol, or . . .

Dear God! It's frightening. They've all vanished. You announce you're going to get married, you wear a ring and . . . and they just disappear. It's not fair. I'm not used to it. How will I stand it? I simply can't. I can't! He just isn't enough. Howie isn't. He's going to bore me soon. I know it. Then what? Well . . . I suppose I'll find a way. Not at first. You have to be careful. So careful. That's a bore, too. But later, when we get into a routine. When we come back from Europe—ah Paris. Paris! When we come back and he starts spending a lot of time at the office with his big deals, his big, big, time-consuming deals—then if Doug or Jeff, the others, aren't moon-eyed over some sweet thing, or full of silly scruples . . . But if they are, so what? There are always new ones. For me there are always, always new ones. And all that money. Money, money, money. Get busy with those big deals, Howie. And I'll mind the mansion, the beach house, the New York penthouse. And other things.

But moving vans! And storage. Ugh! Overholtzer Van Lines and Storage. Coast to coast. Could anything be duller? Why not an airline? Or a hotel chain? Or oil? But no, moving vans. But listen, Andy, it's money. Who cares how? I can just hear Vivian saying that. Good old Viv. I wish she wouldn't call me Andy, though. Sounds so masculine!

Anyway, she's right. Who cares how he makes it?

Imagine his father dropping dead of a heart attack and overnight he's a multi-millionaire running a big corporation. And just turned thirty! Bet he doesn't know the first thing about what he's doing. But he makes it. He makes it! And if he makes it, I . . . But I hope I don't slip anywhere. Not now. God! Wouldn't that be awful. Just awful! Well . . .

There's the door bell. Howie! One more look in the mirror. Wow! Not bad. Viv says I wear too much lipstick. Doug said so, too. He was only sore because of his damn collar. But I don't care. It does things for my mouth. If you have a big mouth, you have to shape it nicely. There!

"I'm coming! I'm coming, darling!" Wish he wouldn't sit on that bell. He's so impatient. Wow! I feel good. And on just one martini. It's so exciting. I'll let him in.

He was wearing that white shantung jacket and blue trousers—the most beautiful blue. What he must spend for his clothes! He wore a darling little bow tie. Red. No, more like crimson, I guess. And black shoes. Patent leather, I think. Honestly, he looked so neat and clean. Immaculate. Just immaculate. I do love men who are tidy and clean. I suppose he had four butlers and a valet dressing him. But it isn't that. It's always something mental with them. They're either clean or they aren't. And he's the most scrubbed looking man I've ever seen.

He stood there in the doorway just looking at me. His eyes swarmed all over me. Honestly, it was positively indecent. But I loved it!

Then he came in and closed the door with this funny look still on his face. He had a little box in his hand and he gave it to me. Orchids. Of course. Now I like that. Honestly, I don't think anyone ever gave me flowers in this crazy California, but Howie. They never think of it. It's more like an Eastern custom. But it seems right to me. It has a certain dignity. And respect.

"You look good enough to eat," he said. "And I think I will."

That was a corny remark. But I smiled. I always smile. He was looking down the front of my dress. You might know. Well ... And then he grabbed me—none too gently. And kissed me. Hard. And, of course, his hand went right where he had been looking.

It made me furious. Just furious! Don't get me wrong. I've been handled before. Lots. And, by experts. But if there's anything that makes me mad, it's to have a guy paw you the minute he comes in the door. You spend an hour, maybe two, making yourself the last word and some maniac tears it all down in about thirty seconds flat.

Of course, I didn't show it. I let him run off a little steam and then I pushed him gently away. "There are some things you should savor," I said in my best manner. "Like good brandy. Sip, darling. Don't gulp. It's a long night. And you've got a good imagination." (He really didn't.) "Keep it working. Till later. Please?" Then I smiled again.

"Sorry, honey," he said. "I got carried away. But if you don't want to set things on fire, don't wear a dress like a blowtorch."

That was the best crack he made all evening. It got me laughing and put me back in a good mood. "You really like it?" I said.

"My God," he murmured. "My God." And then he just stood there looking at me again. And I knew everything was going to be all right. It was going to be a great evening. And I had a great future.

I pinned the corsage to my dress, put on a little white, fluffy wrap I have, and we went down to his car. Car is a bad word. It was an automobile. And there really isn't any name that covers it—ten thousand dollars' worth of Lincoln Continental. And you practically have to be among the four hundred just to place an order for one. Ten thousand dollars! Crazy. Just crazy. There are places where you could buy a small house for that. But to the rich, money is just a kind of dirty green paper you carry around in your wallet because the funny little people demand it. For anything big, you just sign your name on a check. And that must be a bore, too. Well, I'll just have to get used to it. And listen. I learn fast!

So we drove off. Excuse me. Purred off. It was just a few blocks over to Wilshire and Wilshire takes you right down to the Ambassador. He didn't drive fast. I liked that. He's no showoff. He's pretty grown up. I know a lot of men older who are still babies. Heavens. With a car like that, you don't have to show off. And he was very charming all the way downtown. Said a lot of affectionate things—about after we were married, how proud of me he was and everything. You know. But still he had to rest one hand on my knee all the time. Well . . .

Of course, the Grove was crowded. Just jammed! They couldn't call it dancing. They should call it squash. On Saturday night. Howie is a pretty fair dancer. But he didn't get much chance to prove it. Still, we had a perfect ringside table, all reserved for us, and champagne, lots and lots of it, and the crowd began to look pretty good to me. Everything did. The floor show was marvelous—in spots. And altogether, I don't know when I've had such a good time.

Around eleven a funny thing happened. They started a new set and we beat it out to the dance floor so we could have some space. For about a minute. And who should be the second couple on the floor but Viv— Vivian Manbee, my best friend, and Doug. Doug Coleman! Of all people. I was so surprised. And well, pleased. You can imagine. I hadn't seen Doug in so long. For me. We used to . . . Well, he's quite a man. He's kind of slender looking. But that's because he's so tall. About six-two. His looks are deceptive. You can't imagine how wiry and strong he is. He always has that faintly cynical, faintly amused grin on his face. Like Errol Flynn. He looks like him, too. Somewhat. He's terribly good looking, though he knows it and he's a little egotistical. But he wears it well. He's not a bore.

He's my very favorite. I like tall men. Of course, I'm tall myself.

Viv was a surprise, too. Though not so much so. I mean, in a different way. I didn't expect to see her with Doug. She didn't go out much at all. That's because she's not much to look at. I don't keep good looking women around me. We clash. But Doug of all people. With Viv! I was puzzled. But it didn't take me long to catch on.

I had talked to Viv on the phone earlier. She woke me up around noon. I told her that Howie and I were going to the Grove. She was very sweet. But kind of strange. She said, "Well, have a good time, Andy, dear. You never know when you might bump into me."

"What do you mean?" I said. "Of course I'll bump into you. I'll bump into you right here if you'll ever come over and see me."

"I didn't mean anything," she said. "And you know I'll be over. I've been kind of busy lately." (She's a buyer for a department store.) "Things are humming at the mill, you know."

"Stop being a slave and come over and roll in some of my glory," I said.

"Oh, I will. I will," she said. But she sounded kind of funny. Strained.

And then here she was with Doug, who was quite plastered, by the way. And she looked so terribly plain in that red taffeta she drags out for special occasions. Poor thing. Not that it isn't a nice dress. But she has no figure at all. None at all. She's well, let's say it, flat chested. The cupcake sort. And her clothes sort of hang limply on her. She wears suits most of the time. Rather severe for my taste. But she has a pretty face. Well, cute. Sort of impish. She's tiny, you know. She has a little round face and this jet-black hair, short cut and even all around—like you took a bowl and . . . But on her it looks very charming. And she has nice legs for a small girl. And she's very sharp in the conversation department. She's a doll! My very best friend. We used to room together at U. C. L. A.

And after that, we had an apartment in Glendale. We went to high school together and came out West from Buffalo together. We've been very close. Very. Though we've been drifting lately. Since Howie. Of course, it's another world. Marriage.

But what was she doing with Doug? Of all people. Of course I knew. She had called him on some pretext or other, told him I was going to be at the Grove and he had said, "Well let's go take a look at her together." Something like that.

They came over and sat at our table for awhile. Doug offered to dance with me. And he wasn't just being polite. Brother! He was tight of course, and once he got me on the dance floor—well, you could hardly call it dancing. He was unusually blunt about it. We were just swallowed by the mob, it was very dark and we just swayed back and forth, pressing against each other. It was terribly naughty with Howie on some other part of the floor, right within shouting distance and dancing with Viv to be polite. But it was delicious with Doug. Delicious! I had forgotten just how much so.

But then his hands began to wander in the mash and he began to say wild things. Just wild. I had to stop him then. Not because I wasn't liking it, but you know. It was hardly the place. And that made him angry. Just furious. I've never seen him like that. I was really afraid of him. And he used some very choice language, a thing I hate, and among other things, called me a leech and a nymphomaniac. Imagine! He'll get over it. He'll be back. But I didn't know he could be so ugly. I didn't know he had such a furious temper. I thought he was going to choke me right there on the floor. But suddenly, he just left me. Right there on the floor.

It was so embarrassing because Howie and Viv were already back at the table. Doug was standing over Viv, a little drunkenly it seemed. He had her by the arm and was trying to pull her up. He wanted to leave. Viv was willing. Oh, quite. I guess. Poor thing. But she wanted to say good-bye. "Don't mind him," she whispered, as they were leaving. "He's just a big ape and can't find his cage."

Big ape! That isn't what her eyes said. She was probably dying to get him alone. Right then I was a little jealous. Isn't that funny? With my future husband sitting right there. And jealous of Viv is funnier still. It's pathetic.

Anyhow, they left. But not before he turned around, Doug did, and gave me the strangest stare. There was real hatred in his eyes. And the set of his jaw. I really think he cares. But he frightened me. It ruined my mood for the rest of the evening.

That was a very dangerous time for me because after they left, Howie began to ask questions. And they weren't easy questions to turn away. But in the end, I managed him.

We didn't stay very long after that. Howie wanted to go right home. But I knew what was on his mind. It was on my mind, too—in a way. I mean it was on my mind, but not for him. I was thinking about Doug. So I said, "Why don't we run over to the Mocambo for a night cap," just as though running over to the Mocambo had always been duck soup for me. He was a little sullen about it. But we went.

I think it was a little after midnight. I almost expected it to be raining when we got outside because I remember when we left my place the skies were cloudy and it just looked and felt like rain. But driving up Sunset to Mocambo's, it was just plain foggy. Kind of dreary. Those big globs of lights along the Strip looked funny; all kind of hazy and subdued. It was as though these big neon signs were squinting at you with tears in their eyes. Depressing.

I guess it suited my mood, though. The mess with Doug and Viv at the Grove had left a bad taste in my mind. Viv was predictable, but I couldn't figure Doug at all. He had never acted so strangely, so cruel. And the things he said! You think you know someone and then all of a sudden he does something that just gives

you the creeps. He ruined my whole evening. But all
the things I thought about him weren't bad.

Mocambo's was crowded too. It was really much
worse. Because it's smaller. It was just a den of smoke
and noise and tipsy people. I couldn't get with it. Not
at all. Everyone seemed to be acting like children.
Silly. Plain silly. And Howie didn't help. He was still
a little sulky. Half because he still suspected there
was something between me and Doug and half because
I didn't want to go right home from the Grove.

We weren't talking much. Heavens. You couldn't
hear yourself anyway. And we were drinking them
down one after the other without feeling a thing. At
least, I had been cold sober since the Grove and Howie
didn't show a sign that he was in the least bit moved.
I could see the whole damn night was just going to
collapse right in front of me. And that scared me, too.
I couldn't afford to have Howie down on me. I just
couldn't.

So I gave him a big, bright smile and said, "I've had
it. Let's go home." And that did it. He perked up right
away. You would have thought the evening was just
beginning again, that he had just bounced through my
door. I didn't feel that way at all. I was horribly depressed. And I didn't know quite why. But I loosened
up my face muscles and tossed him a couple of fast
cracks that made him chuckle. I didn't want to let it
die.

So we left. The fog was worse than the smog in the
daytime. You could see pretty well, but it was so
gloomy. Howie had his arm around me and his fingers
kept playing a piano concerto. Even that didn't help
distract me. But he kept talking away all the time
and I was grateful because I didn't have to say anything. Just listen and think.

We got home around one-thirty. Howie was still
chattering away about nothing in particular. But I
could sense the undertone of excitement in his voice.
This was the culmination of the evening for him. As it
is with most men. Everything else, the drinks, the

dancing, the nothing talk, is a kind of fill, the band playing the overture while they wait for the curtain to go up. It's that way with me most of the time, too. But not tonight. Not with Howie. That thing with Doug spoiled it. But I'll put on a good show. And maybe I'll get carried away.

He didn't attack me the minute we came in the door this time. But that was only because he knew that now it was inevitable. He played it cozy. He acted as though he had just dropped in for a spot of tea before saying good night. Heavens, a child can see pure daylight through most men.

So I unpinned the orchids and put them in the little box I had saved. Then I took the box and tucked it carefully away in the bottom of the refrigerator. Those flowers probably cost ten bucks and I haven't gotten over being frugal yet.

He followed me out to the kitchen and when I opened the refrigerator he pried up one of the ice trays and began fixing drinks. My mouth tasted god awful and I felt fuzzy. I didn't want another drink. But I took it anyway and gave him a big smile to show him how grateful I was.

We went into the living room and sat down on the couch. It always starts on the couch. At least I don't bother much with the ones where it doesn't. I like a little subtlety even though I know it's a big joke. I like to play the game.

We sipped our drinks for a minute or two. It was rather an awkward silence, a kind of transition I guess you'd call it. Then he said, "Well, sweetie, in eight days," he looked at his watch, "no, seven now—you'll be Mrs. Howard Donald Overholtzer." He fairly beamed. And I beamed back at him.

But translated that meant, we're almost married now. It's just a formality. So you see, it's perfectly all right —what we've been doing, what we're about to do. He didn't know me before. He didn't know me now. I made sure of that. He didn't know he didn't have to pour balm on my conscience. The evening would have finished the same way. No matter what he said or didn't say. Except that if he wasn't Howard D. Overholtzer and if we weren't engaged to be married, I would have been busy when he phoned. I would have been going out with Doug, or Jeff, or Mark, or maybe Ralph Whiting, old as he is.

But I said, "Yes, only seven more days. A week. Isn't that wonderful! I'm so excited, Howie."

"No more work for you, little pal." He was trying to sound breezy about a big thing to him. "You'll have a special maid just to do your hair."

I said, "You know, it's a little too much to absorb all at once, darling." It was. "After standing eight hours a day as a combination model and salesgirl, I'll never get used to it."

He took a drag on his cigarette and looked at me thoughtfully. "You never did tell me," he said, "with your education and breeding, how did you ever get stuck with a job like that?"

He always said I had breeding. Breeding was very important to him. Well, maybe I do at that. At least on the outside. And that's all breeding is, really. To cover up what you're thinking. And so that no one will know you're basically an educated animal with some very vicious instincts. But, to answer his question I said, "Well, like most jobs, it was purely circumstantial. I just fell into it. I didn't type or take dictation and I didn't want to. What a bore! I didn't want to do any of the routine jobs. I didn't want to get into pictures or television, although I had some half-baked offers. I really didn't know what I wanted to do. But I had to earn a living.

"Viv was assistant buyer, then. I'd hate that, too, and she heard about this opening at Annabelle Marvin's. It's a very exclusive dress shop, you know. And I just adore clothes, the pay was about top for that sort of thing, they liked me and I took it. Also, I didn't want to get married—not until I met you, darling." Bro-ther! Was that the truth. Even though I did sneak it in.

"And I didn't want to get married until I met you, angel. You know I really do love you, don't you? Terribly. Insanely."

Well, it was a little overdone, like something out of a "B" picture. But I looked at him carefully and I could tell he really did mean it. I was a little touched. "I know you do, Howie. I just know that."

I wasn't acting and I guess I poured quite a lot into it at that because he looked at me kind of sadly and his eyes shined as though they were getting moist. He has beautiful eyes—terribly dark and kind of latin. And while I'm at it, a wide, sensitive mouth, not those tight, pencil-line excuses for lips. He has delicate features for such a big man, too. The more I looked at him, the more I thought he was a pretty good catch, even in the looks department.

He stared at me for quite awhile and then he turned away, kind of embarrassed. Suddenly he ground his cigarette in the ash tray and said, "Well . . ." Just that one word. But, click! I could just feel him changing gears.

And sure enough, he got up and put out all but one lamp. Then he came back and fell onto the couch, real close to me, just as though it was some kind of accident. Then his arm kind of sneaked around me— just as though he hadn't slept with me the night before. It was pretty cute, though. Once in awhile I like men who are a little uncertain where to start. It gives me a chance to play very dumb.

I was feeling better then. I had begun to be elated again by the thought of all that leisure, all that pampering and luxury in just another week. So I didn't care when his hand began to push down on the top of my dress. I was even a little excited.

"Heavens," I said, teasing. "What are you doing to me?"

"You know perfectly well—by now. And if I'm not doing something to you, we're off to a very bad start." He pushed my dress all the way down. I was afraid he was going to rip it. But I didn't say anything. He could afford plenty more and lots better.

"My God," he said. "Oh, my God! I never will get used to it. I've never seen such a beautiful body. Not in my whole life."

I only smiled. I had heard that before. Plenty. He began to caress me. Then he put his head where his eyes were. And . . . and he bit me a little. Not hard. And, for the first time, I began to feel that queer tingling, that restless ache. I stroked his head. It was a little oily, a thing I don't like. But, by then, I didn't care. So I got up and slowly walked across the room to put out the light. Slowly, because I was naked to the waist and I knew he was goggle-eyed, watching every bounce, every line of my body. When I got to the light, I swung around slowly and let him look at me a moment. His mouth was half open and his eyes turned me every way but loose. My own eyes felt heavy. I reached behind me and turned out the light.

I found him in the dark. I lay down on my back with my head in his lap. He leaned over and kissed me gently. At first. His hands walked over me and did things men's hands have been doing to me ever since I can remember. I had one last thought that made any sense at all. It was that most women don't know exactly what they want until they get it. I always knew. And I said one last thing to him that made any sense. "Do you think we can find the bedroom, darling?"

It was very late, I guess. He was sleepy. He wanted to stay for the night. I said, "No, sweetheart. We'll have plenty of time for that. There are people around here who talk enough as it is. I don't want every frustrated female in the building gawking out the window every time I come and go. Please, darling?" I switched on the bed lamp.

Reluctantly he got up and stretched. He was terribly tan. But those two little white places made me want to laugh. He sat in front of my vanity mirror, very sleepy, his hair sticking almost straight up. He put it right back in nice, tidy order, using my comb—a thing I don't like. His mouth looked so funny—like a clown, with my lipstick smeared all over it. He made a face and began wiping it off with a Kleenex from my box, using my cold cream. It took him a long time. Honestly, he's such a fussy one. But the effect was good when he was dressed. He looked just as glossy and neat as when he called for me.

"I'm beginning to wake up," he said. "I don't want to go home. Not without you. Let's watch the dawn come in over the ocean."

"You mean the smog," I said.

"Come on, honey," he said. "Come on! Where's all that energy?"

"I gave it to you." Funny how they don't crack back at you afterwards.

He said, "I know a place near Malibu where they stay open all night. I can always get in. They have a juke box and pretty fair drinks. Whatta you say? Just for laughs."

"Pick me up this afternoon," I said. "We'll start all over again. Right now, I'm dead." I was. I was so drowsy. He looked disgustingly wide awake standing there by my bed.

"Just this once," he said. "We can go to bed at nine if you like—after we're married."

"No thanks. Tomorrow, honey. Tomorrow." I was half asleep and I didn't have what it took to humor him.

"All right," he said. "See you then."

He sounded mad. But I thought he would come over and kiss me good-bye. I had my head buried in the pillow, waiting. So I could go to sleep. But then I heard the door slam and I knew that was bad. I threw on a robe and went to the window. He was going down the walk. I called to him. He came back under the window. "Changed my mind," I said. "Be right down."

I threw on my gray skirt and a red sweater. I didn't even bother with panties or stockings. I put on a glob of lipstick and clamped my lips together to spread it.

I gave my hair a couple of licks and took my purse to finish the job. For once I didn't care. But in the mirror, I looked pretty good at that.

I ran down the steps to join him. He grinned at me and I took his arm. Even then he was watching how I bounced when I walked. "Some outfit," he said. "You look good in anything." I knew he was right.

It was still awfully foggy out. The mist kind of swirled in the light from those funny lamps where you go down the steps. I was feeling gay again and kind of naughty. We were just about to go down the steps. "If you only knew what I don't have on under this outfi—" I began.

He was turning toward me. And then suddenly his head snapped back as though someone had . . . had hit him right in the face. I don't know if he did that first or if the sound came first—that simply awful, thundering sound, echoing like the street was a canyon.

But the sound didn't make any impression on me at first. I was too busy with him and anyway it seemed to come from quite a way off. After his head flew back that way, I could feel all his weight on my arm. For a second I thought he was pulling some kind of a gag and then some instinct told me he wasn't. Then I thought he was sick and I tried to support him. But he was terribly heavy and I felt him going down. Backwards. He was way over, like when you do a back bend.

All this time he hadn't made a sound. Not a sound. I couldn't hold him. I just couldn't. His arm was slipping through mine and he was falling.

Then I heard it again. That sound. Or did I hear the other thing first? A kind of flat noise, a plop. Like when you strike a rug with a beater. And that was followed by a kind of whine, a singing sound going away, like the string of some instrument plucked.

It doesn't matter. When I heard the big sound, the pounding one, I knew. I mean, I knew the second time. I knew it was a shot. And I was scared. I was terribly

terribly, terribly scared. I think I wet myself. Because I knew about the other, too. About him. By instinct. I wasn't thinking at all.

He had fallen right on his back by that time. I saw the blood on his trousers first. It was, you know— right . . . right around his fly. And I thought, well, maybe . . . But then I looked into his face.

It was gone. Just gone. His right eye. There was just a big, red, oozing hole there. And the whole right side of his face was spread open and covered, just covered with blood. I . . . I've never seen so much.

I was terribly sick. I don't know if in the mind or stomach. I can't stand things like that. Even a finger . . . But that face! That beautiful, beautiful eye!

I straightened up quickly. I squeezed my head in my hands, trying to shut out the sight. I heard myself— yes, I heard myself screaming. It came out without any thought. None at all. And while I screamed, I looked out into the darkness from where the sound had come. Into the fog. I couldn't see a thing. Not a thing!

I began to feel faint. And at the same time panicky. Someone was out there with a gun. Some inhuman maniac. And he must be looking at me as I stood there. Right—at—me! Fear, like a dirty, whispering bat, fluttered around me.

I had stopped screaming. And the silence smothered me then. Just smothered me.

I ran. I stumbled. I ran again. Up the walk. I could feel those eyes on my back, like some obscene animal. The eyes behind the gun. Cruel. Pitiless.

I prayed as I ran. Yes, I even prayed. "Oh, God. My Father. Help me. Save me!" Something like that. And He did. He did! I made it inside. Safe. Safe. I ran up the stairs, trembling so that my legs, my whole body seemed one big convulsion.

I couldn't find the key. I just couldn't, under all that junk in my purse. And then I did find it—and couldn't get it in the lock, my hand was shaking so. Finally, though—Finally!

I slammed the door and locked it. I put out the one

light I had left in the bedroom, running, tripping on the rug. Then I groped around the kitchen sink until I found the bottle. I took it to the big chair and fell backwards, striking the arm. I lifted the bottle. But the cork was still in it. I got it out. I lifted again. The neck of the bottle chattered against my teeth. Some of the whiskey slobbered down my chin. But some of it got down. I gulped deep breaths of air. And after a long time, my heart began to quiet.

I crept over to the window and looked out. He was still lying there. One leg was pulled up and twisted over. He was awfully, awfully still. Then I saw a man come running, half dressed from a building across the way. And then a woman in pink lounging pajamas.

I went to the phone. I called the police. I don't know what silly, incoherent things I said. But I managed the address.

I felt safe after I saw the man come running. And safer still when, after a long time, I heard the sirens. It seemed long. But I couldn't go down again to that. I just couldn't!

Then, when I wasn't so much afraid, I began to be sick. I went to the bathroom. When I came back, I found I could think again.

I didn't feel any pity for him. Not right then. There was too much horror, too much sickness inside me. And I began to be afraid again. In a different way. More subtle. More creeping. I had a quick picture of Doug when he was leaving the Grove. When he turned around. That look. It could kill. I didn't think so then. But yes, it could. It could kill. And that was the beginning of a chronic sickness that I didn't think would ever leave me until they found him. The one. The one.

I sat there in the dark and listened to the sirens drawing closer. And I knew whoever it was had gone. Then, right then, I did have one thought about Howie. I thought, Only a week. Seven days. He had talked about making his will over to me even before. But

I knew it was the kind of thing you just talked about.
And, of course, he never did it. So if it had to happen,
if it just had to, why couldn't it have waited until
the day after? Why couldn't it have waited for eight
days?

Douglas Coleman

I was lounging at my desk in the producer's office over at CBS in Hollywood when the call came in from Vivian Manbee. It was about, oh, half past eleven, I think. I know I went out to lunch shortly after. Saturday morning is pretty slow on TV and I didn't have anything until a rehearsal at two.

I was reading a story in the current issue of one of the big slick magazines. We're always looking for something we can adapt. But plumbers can adapt. It's the story that counts.

It was the usual milk-toast junk about robots who made love in stereotyped phrases, 'He gathered her in his arms and held her tight, his heart pounding in his chest.' (Where else?) And, 'George,' she said, 'do you really think we should? It's so late and we . . .' But then George never did anything anyway, and couldn't, equipment for love-making being restricted to endless arms holding tight and mouths kissing so dryly you could hear the crackle.

I turned the page to an article entitled, Secret Confessions Behind Your Doctor's Door. This article told what couples only think they know and really should know. Here the characters seemed to have all the organs necessary for love-making and a few extras not mentioned in the most sordid novels. The article used such endearing terms as, preliminary love play, premature ejaculation, menstruation cycle, rhythm control, contraceptive and vagina.

I spent a minute wondering about the incongruity of a magazine that ran back to back, a silly, saccharine excuse for a love story, and an article which told fearlessly of the most intimate bedroom pursuits. It was as though in the split second of turning the page, you suddenly grew up and were now permitted to face stark reality.

I tossed the magazine across the room where it teetered on the edge of the wastebasket and finally plopped in.

I lighted a cigarette and stared out the window. The pale sky was cheerless, smudged with dark clouds that threatened rain. I hoped the sun wouldn't come out to laugh at the melancholy and resentment I had been so carefully cultivating for a week, ever since the final treachery of Andrea Lockridge.

The phone rang at my elbow.

"Doug?"

"Unh-huh. How are you, Viv?" I recognized her voice right away. It's low register and has a slightly husky quality.

"Sincere," she said. "I feel very sincere. Doug, what's with you for tonight? I mean, what exciting adventure have you planned that couldn't possibly include me?"

I was surprised. Vivian Manbee is about the most self-contained person I know. Or pretends to be. She doesn't go around hinting for dates.

I had no plans. I hadn't been out for over a week— not since I called Andrea and she told me she was marrying Overholtzer. But I didn't want to go out with Viv. I don't like the type—sharp, pseudo-intellectual, full of acid-tongued observations and about as cuddly and palatable as rye krisp.

"I'm going to hit the sack early," I told her. "Big day tomorrow. TV knows no holiday and . . ."

"Doug. Hold it. Listen! Andy and Howard D. are going to be at the Grove tonight."

"So?" Right away I had stomach cramps.

"So. It's such a peaceful mixture. I need a catalyst. The great welding takes place a week from tomorrow, you know. And, Doug, she doesn't want it. She doesn't really want it. I know her. She'll be miserable. Imagine Andy and Howard D. Overholtzer! Just nothing."

"Nothing but money."

"Sure. But that isn't what she really wants. Not all she wants. She's still a child, dreaming of pink champagne. She'll grow out of it, but she needs help. And I don't have the right equipment. Doug? Are you listening? Doug?"

"Unh-huh."

"Doug. You should never have let it cool. Not even for a week. She needs to be prodded out of it."

"What am I supposed to do—take her out for hot chocolate after he brings her home?"

"You're supposed to be around. Like the tempting bottle just within reach of the abstaining dipso."

"I don't know if I like that crack." I didn't. But it made sense anyway.

"I'm not trying to coddle you, Doug. I'm telling you the truth. I know you've got the sickness. And I've got the key to the medicine cabinet. You better get out your mustache wax and bring all your dangerous charm over to the Ambassador tonight. I think you could stir up a few doubts. Unless, of course, you managed to put out the fire in just a week."

"What time do I pick you up?"

"Now you're using your bean. My place at nine."

"Be there."

"S'long, Doug."

I hung up. I knew Andrea would see through us the minute she caught Viv on my arm. But the drunk knows what the bottle will do to him. And reaches for it anyway.

The rest of the day went to hell after that. I moved in and out of two rehearsals and a show, giving only mechanical attention to such things as musical bridges, dissolves, balops, camera angles, lighting details, sets, boom microphones and the people who made these expensive gadgets function on command so that talent could perform and have its hour of glory.

I was dressed and ready to leave a half hour too early. So I sat around my apartment, sloshing a drink in my hand and composed the evening without being able to compose myself.

Viv wasn't kidding me a bit and she knew it. She wasn't any cupid and her motives weren't hearts and flowers. She didn't like Overholtzer, but she didn't like me much better. She saw Andrea slipping out of her life and Andrea was her life. Vivian wanted to be the sun with the world revolving around her, dependent on her light. But Andrea was the sun and Vivian wasn't even the world. She was merely a minor satelite revolving with a pale glow borrowed from the brilliance of Andrea.

She was a plain, mousy little girl without any physical distinction. She would never have been in the race at all, never entered the starting gate, if it wasn't for Andrea. She could never get a man of her own. But, on the other hand, Andrea had so many, if Viv sat at her bountiful table long enough, she would always come away with a few crumbs (no pun intended) just by being on the scene and being called the Queen's favorite. All this, while she pretended complete indifference. 'Men! Apes in monkey suits beating their chests while hunting for mates with bigger mammary glands and emptier heads. Who needs them?' She did. It was just a pose.

But she had a clever, biting little mind, sometimes brilliant, always eating itself with resentments. And she felt vastly superior, even to Andrea. Though she hid it well and played the roll of mother confessor, adviser and flatterer. Andrea must have been at least partly fooled by this flattery, or else why did she tolerate Viv? She didn't need Viv. She never had. But Viv needed her.

Well, it didn't matter. It didn't alter my situation. Viv was using me and I was using her and we both knew it. She dropped out of my mind quickly. Not so Andrea.

I had met Andrea when she came in to audition for a part on the Theatre of Tomorrow show. Somebody, one of the agency boys, had recommended her, otherwise she wouldn't have been on the list. We don't audition everyone who comes in willy-nilly.

Seated outside the studio there was the usual variety of female talent in the usual variety of shapes and sizes. A girl from my office was checking off the names.

I noticed Andrea right away. In fact, she was the only one I did notice. My God, you couldn't help it. In a room full of people, she'd always be the first one you'd spot. Not that she's loud or cheap. Not that she poses or signals her sex. But she's tall, she's statuesque, with a figure that would flag down the Broadway Limited at seventy, and she packs more appeal in one human form than is really fair to the rest of the female race. On the other hand, she has a quiet manner and a face that's almost demure. This is a combination that I find irresistible.

She was one of the last to audition. Everyone who preceded her, in one way or another, gave a far more polished performance. But being as human as the next one, I didn't tell her we'd keep her in mind. I asked her to wait.

When the list was completed, the talents appraised and noted on cards, I sent for her to come into the control room. The engineer had gone and we were alone. She sat down opposite me, unaffected, composed.

"Miss Lockridge," I began, "I didn't call you back because I can use you on this show, or any other that I know of at the moment. You're not ready. But I think you could be in a couple of years, maybe less— if you're willing to work at it practically all the time. Obviously you own all the good looks you'll ever need. In fact for serious acting, your abundance of physical appeal may be a handicap." I smiled. "You'd have to find some way to tone yourself down. A good many men would find it difficult to listen to you and look at you all at once. You might get in the way of your acting. But you do show a great deal of promise and if you want to work, well, I might be able to give you a short cut or two."

She smiled and I fell madly in love with her mouth.

"You don't know a short cut that would take two weeks instead of two years?" she said.

"No. You learn acting the way you learn piano, writing, singing, dancing or bull-fighting. There's no easy way. I said two years because you have more naturalness than most. But it could take five or ten."

"I'm sorry, then. It's not for me. I just don't care that much about it."

"Good. At least you're not kidding yourself. You have to care about it more than anything else to make a real success of it. It should be an incurable disease. Don't just play around with it. Jump all the way in or stay out. And I guess I don't have to warn you there are a lot of men in this business who will tell you they'll make you an overnight success. They'll try to make you overnight—but not a success."

"I'm pretty well aware of that," she said. "But thanks. You're about the first one who's given me an honest answer."

"If you want an honest answer," I said, "go to a woman. But on the other hand, the answer someone like you would get, might be a little too honest. And speaking of honesty, I did want to meet you as a person even more than as a potential actress. I have a whole filing system full of good actresses. I don't see any rings so I assume that you're not married. Would you have dinner with me tonight?" I could have spent ten minutes more navigating to the same question. But I hate slobbering around.

"I can't tonight," she said. "But I'd love it tomorrow night."

It began just that simply. But I should have known from just looking at her that it would be nothing but complicated from there on out.

So I took her to dinner the following night and we got along right from the beginning. I think that was because she didn't have to play coy with me, no silly fencing with words, no smutty jokes to test her weakness, no sweaty and awkward explorations in the front seat of my car parked on a lonely road.

For the first half a dozen dates we talked about just anything and everything but sex. I left her at the door, kissed her good night and that was it. She wasn't dull anyway. I found her quick and knowing in most areas of conversation, she had a sharp sense of humor, she wasn't spoiled for all her looks and she had a certain gift for being just a damn good companion—warm, but sweetly cynical.

Then one night on the third martini before dinner at the Beverly Hills Hotel, I said, "Look, Andrea, you know I've played straight man from the beginning. I haven't tried to sell you anything but a good time."

She raised her eyebrows. "Of course. It's very appealing. Very."

"I'm in love with you, Andrea. I really am. And I want to find out just how much. If you want to wait a half dozen more dates, it's okay with me. But I want to sleep with you sooner or later and I'd rather it would be tonight. And that's the understatement of the year."

She studied me for a minute through a haze of smoke. Dinner music filtered softly around the room above the muted sound of voices, the rattle of plates, the tinkle of silver. The corners of her mouth twisted slowly upward until I could feel that smile in my groin.

"Why didn't you say so, Doug? Why didn't you say so a long time ago?"

And that was the real beginning of trouble.

Most beautiful women are lousy lovers. This is because they are too self-centered to make the effort. They want only to be pleased, not to please. To be a good lover, you have to give something to the act other than a yawn. Chances are a beautiful woman has been spoiled by a hundred men before you meet her. It will take a fellow egotist almost impossibly out of her reach to arouse her. It is not native to her to be cold, but she has been made so by the boredom of easy conquest. I know this because I have been involved with a good many beautiful women in my business.

As a rule, I have come to leave them alone. The truth is, they bore me, too. I have chosen rather those women who are in the middle between homeliness and beauty. This will usually give them a little humility, without which there can be no real love of any kind. And if they have a reasonable feeling of inferiority, so much the better. Some of the warmest and most lovable people in the world are those who don't feel too secure. They need you. And if they need you, they will give of themselves. Always find someone who needs you.

But I'm sure I must have sensed the difference in Andrea. Otherwise I would have let her pass like the others—a bad bet. Andrea was the best lover I ever had in my life. Her skill was instinctive, not mechanical. It sprang from a dozen insecurities, however concealed.

Yet she was far more to me than a sensual gratification. She was warm. She was tender and affectionate. She had only a surface ego. She was weak—and she needed me.

One night as we huddled close under the covers of her big bed, even our feet entwined so that we touched everywhere, she said, "Darling, sweet, precious Doug— listen to me. No matter what crazy thing I do, no matter what weak and foolish way I go, don't ever desert me. There are times, smug, self-important times, when I think the whole world sits at my feet and waits for my command. And there are people who make me think it's true. But there are other times when I know I'm just a selfish, frightened little girl, if a little girl can be so confused and complicated. The self-important grown-up, the smug one, doesn't need anyone, Doug. But the frightened little girl loves you and needs you all the time, darling. She'd fall in lonely pieces without you. Don't ever leave that one, that little girl."

"If that little girl needs me so much, why doesn't she marry me," I said.

"Because," she answered, "the little girl wakes up in the morning and finds that she's changed back into the smug grown-up who doesn't need anyone."

And that was Andrea—who needed me and didn't. And couldn't be persuaded into marriage. Yet lived and loved with me as man and wife—when the hard, knowing grown-up, smug and powerful, wasn't out with some other man.

Of course, in my blindness and naivety, in my childish trust, I was a long time realizing that these others shared more than her company. They also shared her bed—and made our love, our whispered confidences, our secret and tender affections, a pointless and dirty joke told in a bawdy house.

And then late one night, as it often did so strangely, her phone rang. And she crept out of her bed where she had been warm against me and took the instrument into the bathroom and closed the door. But this time, this once, I grew suspicious. And I listened —behind that door.

I listened to the giggling, the insinuations, the innuendoes. And then I heard, "Yes. Yes, darling. At two. Don't worry, Jeff. He'll be gone . . ." And I knew. And said nothing.

But I waited by an empty lot on that dark side street, where the nearest street lamp is a half a block away, in front of Andrea's. And I saw him come, the tall, handsome one called Jeff, the arrogant looking bastard with the cleft chin, a cleft big enough to put your fist into. He parked his flashy convertible not ten feet away from me on that same dark street and went inside, clear in the light of the antique lamps on her walk, went inside to her bed to lie in the place I had just now warmed for him—and listen to her mouthings about love and needing. And soon after he went to her, I saw her light wink out.

And when, an hour before dawn, he came striding toward my hiding place on the dark, empty lot, whistling his satisfaction, I called to him. "Jeff," I said softly. "That you, boy?"

And when he came to me, I struck him. Again and again. Sobbing, I beat him back against the flashy convertible, beat him helpless and then still sobbing and saying, "Oh, you bastard, oh, you poor, dumb bastard," slowly, methodically destroyed his beautiful features one by one.

Of course I was sorry later because it wasn't altogether his doing. It was Andrea's. And he couldn't know about us. But my wretchedness, my loneliness and hatred in betrayal, had to strike at someone. And he never knew. It was too dark. And I never told him or anyone, because later when I watched night after night and saw that there were many others, I realized that telling him would give me small satisfaction. And after a week in the hospital, he recovered, patched to look almost the same, in a slightly cracked and broken way.

I didn't try to beat up any of the others. It was useless. But I let her know that I had seen and knew what she was. And she cried and promised and begged me to help her. And I forgave her. I even deluded myself that she was passing through a phase, that in the end I would be able to fill all of her needs and she would marry me.

When we were apart, I felt soiled and disgusted and resigned all at once. But when we were close, she was very tender and helpless, always a little contrite, and there was this sweet-sad togetherness. She became an unbreakable habit, an opiate for which I had no cure.

And then she told me about Overholtzer and I began for the first time to hate her, if you can hate and love all at once. This was a different kind of betrayal. Irrevocable. And I was frightened. I knew I was going to have to do something to prevent it. And there was only one thing I could think of. That's what frightened me . . .

Vivian lived over in Glendale. I picked her up a little after nine and we stopped for a couple or so at one of those Melody Lane places in Hollywood. She kept urging me to, "Do something. Do something, Doug, before she marries that dumb sonofabitch for his money and regrets it the rest of her life." Viv always had a very masculine vocabulary which I found a little repulsive. But she kept it to herself unless she was stirred up. "You're the only one who has any real hold on her, Doug. She'll listen to you. Tell her you'll never see her again. She thinks she'll get to sleep with you even after she's married. Convince her, Doug. You've got to!"

I didn't say much. I was feeling morose and sorry for myself. And I was sick of listening to her. I kept pouring them down, getting drunk, thinking, thinking.

We left for the Grove a little before eleven. It was a very bad night—foggy. More like San Francisco than Los Angeles. The streets were shrouded with gray, like folds of gauze, and no wind to blow it away. There wasn't any sky. It was just grayed out.

They were stacked in the Grove like a New York subway train at the rush hour. If Andrea hadn't been at a ringside table, I never would have spotted her. At the table they gave us, you needed field glasses to see anything at all. But after we had a couple of rounds, we managed to bump into them on the dance floor.

I hadn't laid eyes on Andrea for over a week. She had on a pale green strapless that had every male in the room gawking. It was a simple thing, but she could climb into a sack and look complicated. Lord, she looked beautiful. And that's such a weak word to describe her. She made me weak. Literally.

Overholtzer looked as polished as a buck lieutenant fresh from graduation at Benning. He had on a white jacket that looked like ten dollars a square inch, a sweet little maroon bow tie, dress shirt and blue trousers. His hair was slicked back over his big dome like greased patent leather. It matched his shoes. I hated him. I hated his guts, but not so much as a person as an obstacle. I don't think he could tie his shoes without a valet. After giving him a tight nod, when we purposely bumped into them on the dance floor, I ignored him the rest of the evening.

We were about the first on the floor and I had to dance a whole set with Viv. But then on invitation, we joined Money Bags and Andrea at their table. Money Bags was pouring from endless bottles of champagne. He was very gay and possessive, like they were already married. He didn't even notice the storm on my face. But next set I grabbed Andrea and took her to the dance floor. Right away she dropped the pose of being surprised to see me. She knew it was Viv's idea. I was pretty sloppy by then and feeling reckless.

"I suppose Viv talked you into it," she said in my ear.

"You don't think I'd come under my own steam, do you?"

"No. But I'm glad you did. Doug. Doug! Where have you been? I'm not dead. I'm just getting married." She pressed against me.

"Same thing," I said. "Might as well be dead." I pressed back. The shock of being so close to her almost made me black out.

"Aren't you going to come see me? After?"

"No." Her breasts swelled and tortured my chest.

"Never?"

"Never!"

"But, Doug. You know I don't really love him."

"Then why are you marrying him?" There was no room to dance. We fastened against each other and swayed.

"Doug. Don't be naive. It's the only way I can live the way I want to live. But later . . ."

"There won't be any later."

"Doug. I couldn't stand it without you, darling. I need you! Don't you know?"

"You betray me once and for all when you marry him. After I stood by you through all the filth."

"I . . . what shall I do?"

"Ditch him. Right now. We'll go to Vegas. Get married."

"Oh, how I'd love it. But I can't. I've made up my mind. Give me a couple of months. Then come see me. We'll start all over again." Her lips brushed my ear. Where she flowed into me, I felt tumid.

"Bitch!" I said. "You dirty bitch."

"What?"

"You dirty bitch!"

"Doug!"

"So you won't ditch him—even if I walk out of here and never see you again?" My hand caressed her body.

"Doug. My God, Doug. Don't say that. And don't— don't stop!"

"Will you leave him? I love you, Andrea. Jesus, but I love you. Will you leave him?"

"No, Doug. I can't. But later . . ."

"You leech. You goddamned nymphomaniac. Cheap, dirty bitch. You'll wish you had left him." The hand I held at her breast stole up to her throat and squeezed. I saw the terror come into her eyes. I saw that she was going to scream. I left her there on the floor.

I went back to the table. Viv and Overholtzer were already there. Overholtzer looked startled. "Where's Andrea?" he said. I ignored him. "Come on, Viv, we're leaving."

"Why?" she said. "I'm having fun."

"Don't give me any of that," I said. "We're leaving." I pulled her up bodily.

Andrea came back. She looked pale. She sat down. Her eyes pleaded with me. Viv was whispering something to her and Overholtzer was glaring. I yanked Viv away and she came along like a rag doll, looking askew and ridiculous in her limp red dress.

I turned around for what I knew would be a last look at Andrea. She turned away from pacifying Howie boy. The look I gave her was full of all the ugliness and hate of my life. We left.

I drove dangerously in the fog. I squinted to see at all through the added haze of alcohol. "What happened?" Viv's husky voice beside me.

"She refused," I said. "Absolutely. Imagine! For that big greasy slob and his dirty money. He's buying a pro. A lousy, second-hand pro!" I began to sob, quietly.

"Never mind," Viv said. "It's all over and we're a couple of orphans. Let's go home and get drunk together." God! What a pathetic couple we were.

I remember Viv taking me into her apartment and remember how sad-funny we were. I remember her naked, scrawny little body with its child breasts coming toward me in the dark of her bedroom where I lay on her bed. And how she nestled against me crying, and how I held her, neither wanting the other. And how she fell asleep and I couldn't wake her. And how finally I forgot she was even there—and thought of Andrea. And how I got up finally and dressed. Some irresistible voice was whispering that I had to go back to my vomit.

I had to go back and stand in the shadow of that street until she came home.

Vivian Manbee

I JUST SPOKE to Doug Coleman on the phone. He's going to pick me up at nine. Thank God! Because there isn't anyone else in the world who could break this thing up between Andy and Howard. And it has to end. It has to. Tonight. Tonight!

That ass! Coleman. He's been sitting over there all week on his big, fat, wounded duff, nursing his little hurt, doing nothing. Nothing! And Andy on the phone every day telling me she's got to see him, "Just got to Viv or I'll go stark raving mad." Jesus! On a bicycle. It's disgusting. I could puke.

But it could work. Doug could do it. Why didn't I call him before? Because I can't stand him? Or because I still have some of that silly, loathsome pride—pride of the female? Wish I'd been born a man. I'd show this goddamned world. Or if I had to be born a woman, a woman like Andy, instead of a five foot, no inch, no stack bag of bones. Rag mop. Rag mop. Rag mop!

The power. Oh, the beautiful, beautiful power of a woman like Andy. Click clack, click clack, down the street, all eyes turning. Click clack, click clack into the room, all heads bowing. Hail the Queen! Her majesty commands! Lucifer in green hell. Put my brain in her body. How I'd make them run. And simper. And beg!

And I wouldn't give it away either—like she does. My God! She doesn't have to. They'd buy and buy just looking at her. But before I'd make my bedroom like the men's john at Grand Central, I'd be a five-hundred-a-night call girl. And she could get it. A thousand in some quarters. But it's revolting. Those hairy, crawling apes, night after night.

44

The girl is sick. Poor kid. You've got to look at it that way or lose your mind. It's a form of insanity. Absolutely insane. Mad. But then, aren't we all mad? A little. There are times when I stand a little way off and look at myself. And I wonder then. I wonder if I'm not a little strange, too. Of course, I have my reasons. But nobody knows or cares about reasons. Except maybe Andy. And that's why I love her and have to protect her from herself.

Yes, that's right. Nobody knows or cares about you. Not really. No one. They smile and they look you in the eye, they seem to be listening and they come up with some kind of answer. But behind their secret faces, they don't care. You know it. You know that. You know goddamned well. And yet someone wears a little broader grin, gives a little sharper answer, says, "I know. I know, honey, how it is," and you fall into the trap anyway. And you think, here's one, now here's one I can trust. So you get together and you open up a little, not much, and you begin to talk a kind of special language, a little below that surface level where you always wear the mask, and wham! The sonofabitch clobbers you.

You know why? The bastard caught you when your tides came together for a space of time. The tides of circumstance. Nothing else. You flowed along in the same channel over the same rocky bed. And so it appeared that you were one. And then there was an island in the center of the channel. It's a small island, nothing much. An obstacle, a thing involving a small personal sacrifice to go around together. You are willing. But it takes two and you can't. It becomes a point of separation and each takes a side. And then it's too late. Because beyond the island there is no coming together. You flow out to sea and you are lost again in an ocean of loneliness.

Crap! Pure, mawkish crap. There is no room in me for sentimentality or tenderness. The house is empty, brother. All the tear-stained furniture collected by the finance company—Barren Souls, Incorporated. And

I'm thinking in riddles—a sure sign of the meno-pause. Premature menopause at twenty-six.

Of course Andy is another matter. She needs me up to a point (my God, she needs everyone) or she did until Overholtzer. That's why Howard has got to go one way or another. Because I need Andy more than she needs me, though I always make it seem in reverse to her. I need someone to mother. Or is the word smother? She's only two years younger. But she might as well be ten. She only looks and sounds grown-up. She's a sick little girl.

But we're all sick. I'm sick in another way, I guess.

They are all wondering, Coleman, Jeff Slater, Mark Bristol, Ralph Whiting, Bud Masterson, the fair-haired boys of Andy's Greenwich Village, they are all wonder-ing why she would marry a boob like Overholtzer just for his money. After all, Andy doesn't cuddle with anyone who couldn't take her to Ciro's five nights a week and still be able to pay the rent and have money left over for coffee and cakes. None of those guys are penny-ante. They would gladly provide for her in quite cozy fashion. But I understand about this Howard D. Overholtzer business. I alone. Though I can't allow it. Never.

Andy's real name is not Lockridge. It's Lindowski. She comes from the Polack section of Buffalo. The place is loaded with them. Even the mayor is a Pole. And the section she comes from is not exactly high class Polack either. It's a dreary segment of the city with block after block of scabby, frame houses the Negroes would condemn as unfit for habitation. Her father is an underpaid barber, third chair in a three-chair joint and her mother is a waitress in one of the neighborhood cafes when she can stay sober long enough to hold a job. Neither one of them can speak intelligible English.

Andrea made her own clothes all the way through public high school. God knows where they got the rags she wore before that. Her belly was never quite full and she was a stringbean until she was old enough to take an after-school job as waitress in the same joint where her mother worked. She smoked when she was twelve and drank beer when she was thirteen. When she was fourteen, her father used to slip into her bed in the middle of the night—until her mother caught him and he went to jail for incest. That's the kind of background she comes from.

No wonder she changed her name and told Overholtzer her family was dead—killed in an automobile accident. And her hair is not really red. It's that Nordic blonde. She wanted to lose even that mark of her past. I will say, it's a beautiful dye job and few would know.

And she didn't get through U.C.L.A. on a scholarship. She worked after classes in one of those rah rah, juke box and soda jams in Westwood. She was a waitress.

And this is why Andrea Lindowski thinks she absolutely has to marry Howard D. Overholtzer, why she has waited and turned down the others. I think it is some kind of revenge against the world.

And don't worry. I've thought of everything. I sent Howard one of those typewritten, anonymous letters, telling him the whole story. I thought that would certainly do the trick. I couldn't tell him in person for fear he might turn Andy against me. But it didn't seem to faze him. He never told Andy or anyone so far as I know. He's that far gone. But I will say begrudgingly, he's a gentleman, if nothing else, whatever his motives.

Andy has done a lot for me—without really knowing it. I don't think I had a half a dozen dates in my life until she came along. She showed me how to dress and fix my hair and wear makeup. But, most of all, for a long time there, she wouldn't go out on a date unless her guy provided one for me, too—and no jerk, either. Of course, I got in the way of her amours after awhile and she became less and less insistent about fixing me up. Also, we don't room together any more. But I still go out now and then with two or three of her brushoffs and whenever I get blue, she always gets someone for me. Jesus, I hate it. But what can I do?

And, of course, there are parties to which I'm always invited and I'm always introduced as her best friend. It gets very special treatment for me. But, my God, how I wish we were back in the days when we were rooming together.

Anyway, it will be all over next Sunday unless I can come up with something new. If Coleman doesn't work, nothing will. She's simply nuts about him./He could break this thing up and put her back in circulation. Then I don't think she ever would get married. I'm going to see that he's in there trying tonight. If not, this is the end. I've had it. I wish Howard would get run over by a ten-ton truck. Wouldn't that save the day! Because I know the snobbish way Howard and Andy will live. I'll never be a part of their life— never!

My God! It's quarter of two and I'm due at the beauty parlor in fifteen minutes. It won't help. But I just love to have my hair played with.

Doug came for me pretty soon after nine. We drove over to Melody Lane on Wilshire and La Brea, I think it is. I lost count of how many drinks we had. I think he was buying courage to meet Andy with. Or anesthesia for his wounds. I gave him a long commercial pitch about Andy. How he should handle her. He kept nodding but I don't know if he was listening. He seemed sullen and far removed. I felt like he was formulating some kind of scheme of his own.

It was a stinking night. The atmosphere was about like that off-white, sickly paste we used to use in grammar school drawing class. The same color and just as thick. Doug didn't say a word until we got a table at the Grove in the Ambassador. We were supposed to just happen to meet Andy and Howard there. That was my whole plan. Get her together with Doug—and let the hormones mingle.

The joint was jumping with creeps. It looked like a legion convention at the Statler in Buffalo. With my good looks and Doug's pull, we got a table in the last row of the bleachers, right in the end zone.

They had a ringside table and we spotted them in a few minutes. A waiter was refilling their glasses with champagne. They came out to dance and we did a hundred yard dash to bump into them on the floor. Andy had on that green satin job, the strapless one where the bodice line is so low it reveals about a foot of her chest. I'd give an arm for that foot.

Howard looked as scrubbed and white in his two hundred dollar jacket as an interne before his first lobotomy. His face looked like a just-married sign. I wanted to break one of his champagne glasses on a table and jam it into that face and twist it around. There was only one way I ever wanted that man. And that was dead.

We went to their table after the set. Doug was just plain rude to Howard. I was glad. But Howard sailed along in his dream, oblivious.

First thing, Doug asked Andy to dance. Just the minute the music began. That was good. But I had to dance with Howard and he's a terrible dancer, besides which I loathed being near him.

We got back to the table before them. Then a very strange thing happened. A terrible thing for the whole scheme. Doug came back alone. He was positively livid. He had just left Andy right on the dance floor. It was obvious they had a nasty argument. But finally Andy came to the table and sat down, looking beaten, forelorn.

Meantime the Great Man, Howard, was asking silly questions which nobody could or would answer. He was just ignored. Doug remained standing. He grabbed me by the arm and literally pulled me out of my chair. He told me we were leaving and no crap about it. I told him I was having fun. I wanted to stall. He was beyond reason. He was also drunk.

I whispered some remark I can't remember to Andy. I do remember I was going to tell her I'd call her and not to worry, when Doug yanked me with him out of the room. By that time I was feeling pretty sloppy myself.

The rest is just a nightmare, part of it comical, part of it sad. Because Doug was driving dangerously with his load on in that awful paste fog. And he was weeping. Yes, he was. Actually weeping. I kept asking him what happened and he finally told me it was all over. He had asked Andy point blank to break off with Howard and she had refused. Once and for all, he said. It was just over and that was that.

I began to cry myself. I told Doug we would go back to my place and hold a kind of wake by getting drunk. I really did feel a little sorry for him. But much sorrier for myself.

I mixed a shaker of manhattans and we sat on my couch and drank and drank. I couldn't even feel them. But he seemed almost insensible.

The horrible part was when he began to paw me. Not with any passion but like it was a kind of duty. It made me so mad I went crazy. Not that I wanted him. I stripped off all my clothes right in front of him and said, "There, you bastard! Are you satisfied?"

He just looked at me as though he were looking at a store window manikin. Then he stumbled into the bedroom where I found him sprawled on my bed, flat on his back and fully dressed.

I laid down next to him and after awhile his arm stole around me and he held me against him in such a desperate, clutching way, it frightened me. It was like he was drowning and I was the only one who could save him.

He said just one thing, "I'm dead, Viv. My soul is dead. For God's sake finish it. Go get a gun and kill my body."

I didn't answer him. I pretended to be asleep. He

was quiet for a long time. Then he began to shake me. But I faked as though I had passed out. I was afraid he might try to make love to me. I didn't want him to touch me. I wanted him to go and leave me alone.

After awhile he got up quietly and left. As soon as I heard the door close, I got up and dressed. I lighted a cigarette and began to pace up and down, up and down. I was in a boiling frenzy of anger and frustration. As I paced, I picked up anything within reach, a glass, an ash tray, a vase—and flung it crashing across the room where it shattered against the fireplace—the phony Hollywood fireplace.

Andrea Lockridge

IT'S LATE SUNDAY MORNING and my eyes feel like burned out holes in my head. From crying, and also because I haven't had a wink of sleep. Not a wink. And I've been drinking steadily, a thing I don't like, especially in the daytime.

Daytime! Would you believe it? The sun is just burning itself right out of the sky—as though nothing happened last night. Nothing at all. And there is this Sunday morning hush over everything that ordinarily I would just adore; but today makes me want to scream—because there is no one here in the apartment with me—just my thoughts.

I tried turning on the radio. I thought that might help. It's worse! The sound scrapes across my nerves like long fingernails on a blackboard. Besides, the whole dreadful story is on every newscast. They're making a very big thing of it because of . . . of Howie's wealth and social position. And my own name fairly shouts out of the speaker at me like some kind of an accusation so that I want to hide in a closet or somewhere. And I keep thinking of how they'll dig and dig mercilessly into my life, practically getting every man I ever knew out of bed in the middle of the night, asking questions, questions. "Now tell me, sir, exactly what was your relationship with Miss Lockridge?" And someone is going to talk because I must have made some enemies along the way. You can't please them all!

Those detectives with their too polite, too watchful faces, have gone. I can't bear them because everything they say, speaking so softly, seems to have a hidden meaning. I know they'll be back. But now they've

52

gone. At last! They left a uniformed policeman down below at the entrance. He's a sort of watch dog for my protection. I'm glad he's there. He doesn't say much. He doesn't bother me.

He did bring me a paper just now. I called out and asked him to. He got it from a passing squad car. Everyone seems anxious to please me. Now, anyway. The paper was an extra. Of course, it was right on the front page in bold type. I was going to read it. But then I saw the picture—that gruesome thing called Howie Overholtzer—by me. They refer to him as "the body," in that impersonal way, as though he never was a human being. But when I saw the picture it brought back the whole sight in such horrible detail that I just dropped the paper to the floor like some unclean thing and never did look at it again. I wouldn't let them take a picture of me. But I suppose they'll dig one up somewhere anyway.

After the police cars came last night, I watched from the window. I wouldn't go down there. I absolutely refused. I called to the police from the window and asked them to come up. Not long after the police arrived, reporters with their hungry cameras and pencils, their disinterested eagerness, knocked on my door. I told the police I positively would not be interviewed or allow any pictures—of me. They took hundreds of the . . . of Howie. The reporters were kept out. But they got the story, my story, anyway. Second hand. From those detectives.

After the police left, it got very busy outside. I watched this from my window, first turning out the lights and making sure the door was locked. A big crowd had gathered by this time and their faces were —I don't know—obscene. Just obscene. They had an awful lot of light down there and I could see very clearly. You'd think it was some kind of lawn party with a degrading floor show the way those people gaped. And now and then you would see someone smile. Actually smile! Not really a smile. A kind of sly parting of the lips.

Right on the heels of the police cars, an ambulance —or whatever—came screaming up. No wonder there was a mob with all that noise. But the ambulance just stood by for a long time while photographers took pictures and those plainclothes detectives examined the ground and the street, not mine, but the dark side street that comes into mine. That must have been where the murderer hid. My God. Oh, dear God!

Then they put Howie on a stretcher and covered him with a sheet. It was when they began to carry him away that I lost all control. I was hysterical. I just sobbed and sobbed. And nobody, absolutely no one, to comfort me.

Then the police cars and the ambulance and the detectives, all but the uniformed officer, went away. And after the crowd had simply gorged themselves with the sight of the . . . the blood on the walk, they went away, too. It was still dark. And all of a sudden it became hushed. Unbearably quiet.

That was the worst time. The worst of all. I had wanted them to go. Just go and leave me. And then when they were gone, I wanted them back. In a way. But now that they were gone and I was alone in that dark, empty apartment, I began to have something like delirium tremens. I was shaking all over and my mind kept skipping from one picture to another, each thought with a different emotion. First, I would live through that terror when I first knew Howie was hit and I would hear that sound, the big, cruel, gun sound smashing out of the night, the bullets striking him and whining off somewhere. And then I would see him lying there, the eye gone, just gone, nothing but an oozing space, the red blood against the white of his face and all over that immaculate jacket, almost . . . almost matching his bow tie. Repulsive!

And then I would step back a way and see him differently—a man called Howie Overholtzer lying dead on the ground, a man who had slept in my bed and nestled like a baby against me, and smiled and laughed just a little while ago, telling me I'd be Mrs. Howard Overholtzer in just another week. The millions I could have had, to say nothing of the social position. What a loss. What a waste! I'll never be anything now. And it made me feel terribly, morbidly sorry for him and for myself at the same time and I would cry until there were no tears but just a dry gulping coming out of me.

And then I would see myself running and stumbling and praying and I would feel the evil of that gun on my back, the insane cruelty of the eyes behind it out there in the dark. Insane! Pitiless!

And I would wonder whose eyes they were. What kind of a man could do such a thing? Did I know someone like that? Or was it a stranger? I had this creeping feeling it wasn't. No! There was some inhuman, ugly, but terribly personal hate behind that gun. I knew it. And I was afraid. Scared like you could never imagine in your wildest dreams. Shaking on the inside even when I wasn't shaking on the outside. A kind of sickness. A violent sickness.

But who? Doug? Maybe . . . No. Not Doug! I didn't want to believe it and I couldn't. Now I would need Doug more than ever. Jeff Slater? Was it you, Jeff? Or Mark or Ralph? Bud? Or was it some man I had been out with only a few times and then dropped? Someone nursing a small cancer of hate until it got so big it had to kill the nearest thing to me. And the most valuable. That seemed most likely. But then you never know. You never know the twisted, tortured things that go on inside people you see almost every day.

But now was he satisfied? Or would he want to kill me next? Or had he intended to kill me all along and hit Howie by mistake? I don't know! I don't know! But until they catch him, I'll never be able to close my eyes. Never!

I called Viv just now. She was shocked. Just shocked! She swore something awful. And then she was kind. So very kind. She said that Howie was such a wonderful man, that she had always been fond of him and that she had been just overjoyed that we were going to get married and have such a fine future. It made me cry all over again.

She's so strong. Viv. She says not to be afraid, that she's going to take care of me and protect me. Well . . .

She's coming over right now. She's going to stay with me for awhile—at least until they catch that awful man. I only have this one double bed I'm lying on now. And I can't ask her to sleep on the couch and I don't want to sleep there myself. But she's such a little thing and she won't disturb me. She won't take up an inch of room. And anyway, I'm not going to sleep. I don't think I'll ever sleep again.

Of course if Viv comes over, then that's the end of . . . How can I think of *that* now? But I know when I calm down, I'm going to be wild. Just wild! All this pentup fear and sorrow has to have an outlet.

Of course, I could send Viv to a movie or something. Then Doug could . . . But suppose he's the one! Well then, Jeff. But suppose he's the one? Oh, this is awful. Awful! What am I going to do?

What will I do?

Jeffrey Slater

IT'S MONDAY MORNING and I should go down to my office in the boat yard, or at least check and see if there's anything doing at the pier. But I've just been reading a second newspaper account of how Overholtzer got his head shot off, and I suddenly don't feel like it. Of course, I'm not thinking of him, but of Andrea. So I won't go anywhere until I can get in touch with her. What's the use of owning your own business if you can't take off when you want to?

I own this boat yard in Santa Monica. Slater Boat Sales and Service. We have the Chris Craft line and we also sell Evinrude outboard motors and a variety of small open boats. We do a lot of repair work, motor overhauls and general hull patching, caulking and painting. We sell used boats on commission and we rent space to owners who want to park their boats in the yard during the winter months.

Then down at the Santa Monica Municipal Pier, we have a shop where we sell fishing tackle and boating supplies, doing a good business with outboard rentals in the spring and summer months.

It's nothing gigantic, but altogether I realize a nice profit. Luckily, I was boat-happy from the time I was a kid, so I got an early start. And at thirty-three I'm in good financial shape. Last year the business grossed just under a hundred thousand. Of course, there's a lot of difference between gross and net. But I always use the gross figure. It sounds pretty impressive, you know.

It would be a lot more convenient if I lived in Santa Monica and also I would be close to Andrea. But somehow Santa Monica seems a little second rate to me and I live here in Malibu, high on a cliff, over-looking the ocean. Malibu is about ten miles from Santa Monica along the Coast Highway. It only takes me fifteen or twenty minutes. Then from Santa Monica, it's about thirty minutes to Hollywood and forty-five minutes to an hour into Los Angeles, depending on traffic.

I have a small, California ranch-type house here on this cliff. It has picture windows from which you can see up and down the coast for miles. It's beautiful. I think especially so at night when you can see that firefly bow of lights all the way to Palos Verdes.

Wilma allowed me to keep the house when we got the divorce because she knew how much I loved it. Wilma is not aggressive about money or property any-way and I believe she was more hurt than angry when I asked for the divorce. She wasn't vindictive or anything like that. And there were no children to make a federal case out of it. Still, in a state like California, she could have caused me plenty of trouble. She could have taken half of everything I own. Even if she didn't want the money or the property, she had a marvelous chance for revenge. But she was soft. She didn't take it.

This is a quality I don't particularly admire. This softness. Unless, of course, I'm on the other end of it. If anyone does something to hurt me, seriously, I mean, I want to step right down on him and crush him like a dirty bug crawling out from under the sink. And I do. Because this messy thing they call life is trouble enough from the cradle to the grave without some pig-brained excuse for a human being giving you a shove closer to the cliff. Any goddamned bastard who shoves it in me is going to get it right in the chest just as soon as I can take it out of my back.

I was married a little over five years. I'm used to having someone around with enough mental and phys-ical equipment to be good company. I don't like being alone. But after Wilma left, I wasn't especially lonely because I had expected that Andrea and I would be married shortly after. This shows you how much you know when you're going to get the Hollywood-type stab and twist between the shoulder blades.

Andrea and I had been going together for some time off and on. That is, any night that I could stake a claim before one of the hungry mob from the wolf pack beat me to it. Though, actually, I think Andrea went pretty steadily with me long before any of the present regulars established themselves in her kingdom. I started dating her when she was fresh out of U. C. L. A. Doug Coleman, Mark Bristol, Bud Masterson, Ralph Whiting and Overholtzer came quite awhile after. But, of course, in between there were always a good many of the one or two night stand boys, the names of whom I never knew or have long since forgotten. I'm only saying that even from the standpoint of longevity, she owes me the most loyalty. I can hear her hollow laughter at the mention of such a word. Loyalty.

In any case, Andrea was quite obviously in love with me from the beginning. I've been around too much to be fooled. I'm a pretty damn good-looking guy, if I do say so, and I've had a lot of experience with women. And women run pretty much from cold to lukewarm—unless they're in love with you. They're not really sexual. Sex is a by-product of a strong emotion with them. Love. Or whatever they believe to be love. And Andrea is for me, and me alone, of course, the most passionate woman I have ever known. She's positively—well, I don't find words to put it decently. And this, to say nothing of the fact that she tells me every time I'm in her arms, in the most endearing terms, how much she loves me. I don't want to go into that kind of sacred sentiment, but take my word for it that it's a foregone conclusion she loves me and always has.

Oh, I know. It doesn't make sense, it doesn't hold water when you consider that she goes out with so many others. Not on the surface. But you have to know

Andrea. That's the thing. She is one of those beautifully delicate flowers that needs more than one drop
of water to survive. Naturally it's just plain female
vanity. She needs a lot of attention, a lot of people
dancing around her. I don't excuse it. But I do know
that it is just a passing phase. In many ways she
is just a rather delightfully spoiled child. She'll grow
up suddenly and wonder what she ever saw in any
of them. Meantime it's one of the penalties you pay,
as gracefully as you can, to that rare thing, a truly
beautiful woman.

But this extreme popularity is natural with one of
her type and has nothing to do with her virtue. I've
always been able to comfort myself with that. She
was a virgin until the night that I gently took it from
her. And I believe her when she says that there was
never anyone else and never will be. In that regard, I
know women. I can't be fooled.

Nevertheless, Andrea is a very selfish and cruel
person. Now that she is free again, I am going to
forgive her openly and marry her. But secretly I'll
never forget or forgive what she has done to me.
There will come a time when I will find a way to
crush the arrogant, smirking, all powerful, do-as-I-
damn-please spirit within her. She'll be down on her
knees with humility—begging. I won't forget. Never.

Andrea has a money lust equivalent to her sexual
lust for me. And that's plenty! In fact it would be
too obvious for me not to admit that this money need
sometimes goes beyond her desire for me. I knew of it
all along. I sensed it in her conversation, her every
act. And I catered to it.

She must have imagined that I was well off from
the very beginning because she came down to the
pier with that angular, bony excuse for a female,
Vivian Manbee, (I can't stand that one) looking
for one of those mob-scene all-day boats to go fishing.
I don't think it was her idea. She's not the type. But
Manbee wanted to go and she tagged along.

They came into my salesroom on the pier asking

questions. I told them they were too late. Both of the boats had gone out. It was a pretty busy day for me and I didn't get ahead by fooling around. But I got one long look at Andrea and work didn't seem important at all. So I turned the operation over to one of my flunkies and took them both out on my yacht. I had forty feet of the sleekest Chris Craft cruiser you ever saw. Actually, I used it as a demonstrator. It was for sale. But I didn't tell them that. I've sold it since.

Andrea was pop-eyed when she saw it. She was very impressed. I don't know what Vivian thought because I didn't really look at her or listen to her the whole day.

There's no point to the story except that while Andrea must have been already sold on me as a person, the yacht spoke for my financial status. I did make it an exciting day for them. I trolled along the coast and picked up some "snakes," barracudas, doing all the dirty work and letting them reel in. Then I went down around Paradise Cove and found some blue sharks on the surface, took one of my high-powered rifles and popped them right to the bottom for their benefit. Andrea's, I mean. It was a very successful day. Because I caught Andrea—a very elusive type of game.

Later I showed her the whole layout from pier to boat yard. She asked a lot of questions that were quite obviously leading to my income. I dropped a few hints, nothing specific. I knew she wasn't a gold digger but wanted to be well provided for. I don't think she's ever had much, though she has a regal bearing and the manner of a New York debutante.

Later, when she was obviously in love with me, I let it drop about the yearly take, giving her only the gross figure, one hundred thousand. She was positively overcome, though she tried to conceal it. Then I told her I wanted to marry her and it took her a day or so to say yes. I knew she just wanted to dignify herself in my eyes.

Then—then I told her I was married. She was so shocked I quickly added that however, I was separated

and it would only be a matter of two or three months
before my wife got her divorce in Vegas.

I finally satisfied her and went through some terrible
scenes with Wilma until she did actually pack off for
Las Vegas. I felt just guilty enough that I gave her a
fairly large amount of cash and fixed alimony at a
hundred a week without being asked.

And would you believe it! A week before the divorce
came through, Andrea met this Overholtzer, who was,
of course, a millionaire, and called it off with us. She
wanted to continue seeing me, but she wasn't "ready"
for marriage and didn't know if and when she would
be.

The sad part is that I really have nothing against
Wilma at all. She's pleasant and intelligent, very com-
panionable, and though she doesn't come close to
Andrea for looks, she's very attractive. Very. I would
have gone on with her indefinitely. But I fell in love
with Andrea in such an all-consuming way that I was
and am a little out of my mind about her.

I got right on the phone to Wilma. If I couldn't have
Andrea, I wanted Wilma back. She was cool but very
polite, even kind. But she wouldn't hear of it. She
said she had been through too much and after long
consideration, she felt that our marriage had been a
mistake to begin with. No amount of pleading and ex-
plaining could persuade her. She got her divorce. And
now I don't have her but must send her a check every
month. And I don't have Andrea, either. Or didn't.

I continued to see Andrea—in the most intimate
way, still trying, still hoping. She kept seeing Overholtzer and I think, a few others. She was very secret
about her dating, being sure not to get any lines
crossed or so much as reveal whom she had been out
with, though, of course, I knew generally. Sometimes
she would have an early date and then see me on the
sly later at her apartment. She always instructed me
to call first if I wanted to come over late.

One night I did call her late. I think it was about a
month before she finally became engaged to Over-

holtzer. She told me someone (no name mentioned) had dropped in for a nightcap but that she would get rid of him and I was to come over at two A.M.

This secret rendezvous business kind of tickled me and I did go over that night, or morning, and stayed quite awhile. She was just ravenous for me and practically agreed to marry me.

I left her place around four or five. I don't remember. I had already come to the conclusion that Overholtzer had preceded me, though I couldn't get it out of her. I was just about to unlock the door to my new Olds convertible when a man's voice called me. By name!

It was very dark on this side street and I couldn't see him clearly. But I walked toward the sound of the voice and the dim outline of a man about my size. The voice sounded familiar. In fact, I think I knew even then it was Howard Overholtzer. I had met him at several parties given by Andrea and hated the bastard first look at him. He was one of those conceited nincompoops who couldn't hold a job as stock clerk but climbed to the top over his father's grave.

Anyway, I knew him. Well. His voice, his build. I have a very good memory for voices and I knew his flabby outline. I wasn't fooled by the darkness at all.

But I was kind of shocked hearing someone call out to me in the dark at that time of the morning. I was stunned and slow to realize who it was. So I walked toward this man in all innocence and friendliness.

When I got close enough to guess from the look of him that it must be Overholtzer, he swung at me. The blow knocked out two of my teeth and, of course, caught me completely by surprise. Otherwise, I would have literally killed him with my bare fists.

But before I could recover, he hit me again. I fell back against my car, almost unconscious. Then he really took advantage of me. Clutching my coat with one hand and using the car as a prop to hold me up, he half beat me to death. He literally chopped my face to ribbons. It was the most inhuman and disgusting thing one man could do to another.

Of course I lost consciousness very quickly and didn't feel a thing after the first few blows. I found out later that a man and his wife returning late from an all-night party, discovered me lying practically in the gutter. They took me to a hospital where I didn't even regain consciousness for hours.

It took the most skilled surgeon to sew my face back together again. Then I was in the hospital for about a week. The surgeon did a beautiful job considering, and a dentist made me a bridge. But my nose was broken and will never look quite the same. There are scars under my eyes that still show, my lower lip has a slight droop and my jaw dislocates with any exaggerated movement of it.

And the worst was yet to come. I was hardly out of the hospital a couple of weeks when Andrea told me she was going to marry the dirty bastard—so that all of my agonies and plans had been for nothing.

Do you think I forgave Mister Overholtzer? That I have forgiven him, even now? I'd like to run a spear through his grave . . .

I finally got through to Andrea. Just now. I had called her Sunday as soon as I read the first, sketchy account in the paper. But that bitch Vivian Manbee answered and said very rudely that Andrea wasn't taking any calls. And she knew who it was because I told her.

I called several times this morning, but the line was always busy. I finally got through to her personally a few minutes ago. It seems that Vivian is at work today and Andrea is taking her own calls. That's a break at least.

Andrea was very strange on the phone. She seemed pleased that I had called in one breath, and wary in the next. She was hesitant and vague. She accepted my sympathy in a flat, tired voice. When I asked if I could see her, she said, "I'd like that. But well—I don't know. Maybe sometime."

When I pressed her to know when, she kept saying, "I don't know. I don't know."

Finally, I got it. I said, "Well, Andrea, why don't you come right out and ask?"

"Ask what?" she said.

"Ask if I did it."

"Did what?" If a voice could go pale, her voice had gone pale.

"Murdered him," I said clearly, enjoying myself.

"Oh!" she said in the most startled way. "Oh!"

Then there was a long silence and she said, "Well?"

So I said, "Of course I didn't, darling! Do you think me capable of that!"

"Well, no, but . . . Oh, Jeff. Jeff! I'm so glad you said it. I've been so horribly, horribly frightened."

"Then you will see me?"

"Yes. Yes!"

"When?"

"I don't know. I don't know! But, Jeff?"

"Yes?"

"Say it once more."

"I did not kill Howard Overholtzer," I said. "I was miles away at the time and I've never so much as laid hands on him."

That's what I told her—to her vast relief. But do you think if I had killed him I would tell her?

Or anyone?

Andrea Lockridge

Viv Manbee has moved in with me and I feel ever so much better. She's such a comfort! You would never think that under that breezy, hard-boiled veneer she assumes, there could be such a world of understanding and sympathy.

Last night, (Monday night) we were sitting in my living room having a drink and talking about . . . about Howie. For the first time I was telling all of what happened and how I feel about it. Thank God, I have no secrets from Viv.

Also, we were talking about my dismal future and then about death, a thing I don't understand, and such talk leads always back to Howie. Suddenly I began to cry. Uncontrollably.

Viv put her arm around me and said, "This has been a terrible, shocking experience for you, Andrea dear, but you will get over it. And the sooner you do, honey, the sooner you can take advantage of it. Because overnight you're going to find that you've grown up. And grown-ups have a hard shell they crawl into that protects them from the emotional fairy stories that life is a carnival where handsome men with white-collar-ad-smiles are giving away cotton candy, ice cream, diamonds and free rides to pretty little girls with thirty-eight-inch busts.

"No, Andy dear. Life is a dirty side-show on the road to oblivion. And the smiles of the dirty little men behind their gaudy counters are sly. Because they know the cotton candy and the ice cream you will earn with your sweat and your tears will give you a tummy ache and leave you still wanting. The diamonds will be phony. And the only free ride is the last one."

Honestly! Viv is so deep. And so funny and bitter all at the same time. I don't always understand what she's driving at, but I have the feeling she's usually right. Anyway, I don't know what I'd do without her —especially now.

Well, this is Tuesday and they haven't caught him yet. It frightens me. I have this uneasy sense about it. I have the feeling they aren't going to catch him and that he has some kind of sickness in his brain that waits to flare up again like epilepsy or something. And why do I have this horrible feeling there is no cure but me? I mean, no real relief until . . . until I am dead also. If it wasn't for Viv being here, I think I'd be in a mental institution.

Those two detectives were around again today, going about their business with those bland faces and soft voices, never shouting and accusing the way they do in the movies. They seem like post-graduates taking notes on a zoological expedition.

One of the men's names is Brehmer—Lieutenant Brehmer. He's a big, square man with rimless glasses and a crew haircut. Imagine! He must be forty. He does most of the talking. He has taken a list of all my closest men friends and keeps asking if there are any I have forgotten—even years back. But he doesn't tell me who he's talked to or what they said. It makes me wonder . . .

I get more information from the newspapers. They imply that perhaps Howie had some business enemy and that the police are checking on anyone Howie fired when he took over. Silly! A child could look at me and know the motivation was jealousy.

I keep saying I know nothing about the fight, the beating Jeff took early that morning. Jeff himself believes it was Howie and so I go along and say, Yes, Mr. Overholtzer was the one who came up for a nightcap and it must have been him. I'm sure Doug did it, but I must protect him. I think Doug is capable of beating up Jeff in a jealous rage. But I know he couldn't kill anyone in cold blood. I have to know that. I need my darling Doug. But on the other hand, what if he? . . . I mustn't think about that. I mustn't!

I went out for the first time today. After all, I can't seal myself in a tomb. And I had to get some groceries.

It was necessary to go past the place on the walk where Howie practically died in my arms. There was still a large, faded stain where he lay. When I saw it, I nearly fainted, turning my head and hurrying on. Wouldn't you think they would have the decency to scrub that place clean? But you can't scrub a picture out of your mind.

The uniformed policeman who has the day watch walked with me to the store a couple of blocks away. His name is Mike and he's a cute blonde boy with freckles and this shy smile. The shy ones don't fool me with their smiles. I watch where their eyes go. Anyway, Mike says he doesn't think they are going to leave a man on duty after today. They don't feel that any harm will come to me. The killer was only interested in Howie. I wonder. Oh, dear God, I wonder . . .

Mike carried my packages up to the apartment and stood talking to me in the doorway. I knew he wanted to come in and I wanted him to so badly that I became a little dizzy. I finally had to be rude to him to cover up and practically shut the door in his face. I can't afford to start that with just anyone. If I took up with him, then next it would be that cute one at the drugstore who can't make me a decent soda because I make him nervous, and then maybe some sweet little delivery boy—or even the milkman! That would be the beginning of the end. That would be when I would wish that shot would come out of the dark and take me. Because once you start you never get rid of them and you become like a bitch dog in heat, the whole neighborhood is alive with animals on the prowl for you.

I know this because about a year ago there was a delivery boy who came once too often and at just the right time. I never could get rid of him or shut off his obscene remarks when I wouldn't give in again. He kept phoning at all hours with his dirty suggestions. I finally had to move. And there again, I wonder. What was his name? What was his name?

He was just the kind who would be hiding somewhere in the dark, looking into windows and watching girls undress with his pants unzipped. A little crazy. A little twisted. If you knew his secret mind. What was his name? I've simply got to give it to the police. I can always deny anything a person like that might say about me.

Actually, the only men I feel at all sure of are Doug and Ralph Whiting. Yes, I'm certain of Ralph. He's so much older. I mean, I hate these juvenile delinquents my own age, but Ralph is about forty-one. And though we've been terribly intimate, when we're just talking I feel like he's kind of a father to me. Because as far as I'm concerned, I never had a father.

Ralph is shorter than most men I date. With high heels I even top him a bit. But he has a very rugged build, kind of stocky. He has pure gray hair, almost white, and a face that looks like it's been set on fire. He doesn't seem to brown—he just stays sunburned. He has very clean and rather powerful looking features with the kindest azure eyes you ever saw. He is kind. One of the kindest men I know. And the wisest. He runs so deep you could drown talking to him—and love it. As much as I love Doug, I'd be even more sure of Ralph—because I've never seen him out of control. He's a walking man of distinction ad and twice as poised.

I talked with Doug today—as I have every day. He's coming over tonight and we're sending Viv to the movies. I'm so excited! I've been making love to him in my mind all day. It seems like forever since we . . . But I don't think Viv approves at all. She gave me the strangest look. And she grew very withdrawn. Well . . .

And Jeff phoned Monday. I don't know about Jeff. He must have despised Howie. But I'm going to see him sooner or later. I just know it. Ralph called, too. In fact they've all checked in now. Makes me feel kind of good. In a way . . .

Viv has already gone to the show and Doug will be here any minute. One thing that frightens me. I notice that the night policeman didn't come on duty. They must have decided to end the watch sooner than Mike expected. But I don't care. It's more private. And certainly Doug has no reason in the world to want to harm me. Or does he?

My God. Oh, my God! Why do I always feel right on the edge of a scream?

Ralph Whiting

THE MOST TRAGIC THING has happened. Howard Over-holtzer was shot down in front of Andrea's like a common gangster. It's foolish to feel sorry for the dead since we are all sentenced to die at some indeterminate time the very day we are born. And happier dreams than these can ever be may lie beyond. If not, what pain is there in oblivion?

Yet I do feel sorry for Howard since he was a man who had everything to live for. And didn't know it. One of the penalties of the so-called idle rich is that in the midst of the most astonishing plenty, they are always a little bored. In the end, he would have been bored with Andrea, too, though by then the damage, to her, would have been complete.

No, I am most sorry for Andrea because her suffering was not ended by a scrap of lead and brass, caliber .30-06, but must go on and on because it is mostly self-inflicted.

I was returning from the beach at Laguna when I heard the news over my car radio. I had been visiting overnight with my mother who has a cottage there by the shore. She is seventy-seven now and is living out her old age in this charming little place I have at last been able to provide for her.

It was late Sunday afternoon and I was returning to my home in Brentwood when the news came over the radio. There had been some music preceding the newscast and as usual I was deep in thought. As I grow older, I have come to live more and more in the mental realm and I have a fine time chatting with myself. Consequently, I didn't realize at first that I was hearing the most startling bit of news of my whole life until I caught the name Andrea Lockridge. Until then I had thought the announcer was just warming his audience to another of those almost daily shootings and I wasn't half listening.

Of course, when I heard her name I grabbed the volume control and turned it way up, listening to every word. There wasn't much, but that was plenty. The newscaster simply said that millionaire, Howard D. Overholtzer, had been shot dead in front of the residence of Miss Andrea Lockridge, his fiancée, by an unknown assailant. The item went on to say that the shooting had taken place at approximately three A.M. Sunday morning as Miss Lockridge was seeing Overholtzer to his car, concluding that Miss Lockridge was unharmed and that the police had no clue to the identity of the killer but were undergoing an intensive investigation.

I pulled right in to a gas station and called Andrea immediately to see if I could be of any help. Vivian Manbee, one of the most wretched human beings I know and the most starved for an ounce of love and affection, answered the phone. She was anything but cordial. However, I promptly forgave her because I knew she must be under a severe strain and was only trying to protect her best, perhaps the only real friend she has.

Vivian said that Andrea could not be disturbed and was not in the least interested in talking to anyone for some time to come. No, there was nothing I could do, but had I checked with the police? When I asked why I should, I was told the police were interested in talking with anyone who might have the slightest motive.

I still managed to remain objective and told Vivian that I would be very happy to talk with the police and would give them a call from my office in the morning. She hung up without so much as a good-bye, although I have taken her out frequently as a kindness and not with any feeling for her other than sympathy.

I drove on home in great distress and with an overwhelming sense of sadness—because I knew that if

Andrea needed anyone at that moment, it was me. Without false modesty and yet with humility, I want to say that I don't believe anyone in this world understands Andrea in the way that I do. Nor can anyone love her as much. No one truly loves without understanding and in understanding, forgiving. Actually, to understand and to forgive are one and the same.

I met Andrea and her little friend, Vivian, when they came into my Brentwood Real Estate office looking for an apartment for Andrea. It soon became apparent to me that the two girls had had a fight which they had recently patched. Not that anything was said. I just got that impression.

They had been living together in an apartment in Glendale, a place they had moved to shortly after graduating from U.C.L.A. because the rent was reasonable. Now, however, Andrea wanted to maintain her own apartment so that she would be closer to her work in Beverly Hills. This was the reason given. But I gathered from a quick study of each of them that the decision was Andrea's and that poor, unattractive little Vivian was slightly in the way of Andrea's immense popularity. It seemed a very sad thing to me after I got the drift of it.

Andrea wanted to live in Santa Monica close to the water. I had a few very fine Santa Monica listings and I personally drove the girls around until they found just what Andrea wanted. It was a very nicely furnished place just a couple of blocks off Wilshire and not a dozen blocks from the Pacific. I was able to get Andrea moved in that very day. Both girls had taken time off from work to explore.

My wife of some fifteen years, Nita, had died six months before of cancer. We might have had one boy who died during a Caesarean. So you see I was very much at loose ends. I had a comfortable home in Brentwood with no companion but a cocker spaniel. Dogs are much more lovable than most people. But obviously there are needs they have never been able to meet.

I am not a lonely person by nature because I have a great deal of self-containment and don't require much outside amusement, preferring to talk with myself or the writer of a thoughtful book without the necessity of being burdened with his far less objective personality. All people are interesting in one way or another but most are not good companions because they are lazy thinkers and have not grown much sharper through the years than the chalk of their grammar school blackboards.

As for women or girls, I have usually found the tax of a long evening across from vacant faces and empty minds too great for a dubious promise of their full bodies. And this reward three or more tedious dates later, complete with hypocritical mouthings about morality.

I don't mean this in the smug way that it sounds. I just think the whole thing is a sham and a silly game not worth the effort—in most cases. On the other hand, if a female has enough in the head and especially in the heart, I am willing to let that be a reward in itself.

Andrea was another matter. She came at a time when I was beginning to feel some sharp edges of loneliness and desire. She is not the deepest person in the world. But she has a quick mind, a sense of humor and more heart than most people give her credit for. Also, she fits these qualities into the damndest, most appealing package man ever laid eyes on. Her attraction is as real as her sensuality. She's not a blank stamped from a beautiful mold. Also, she doesn't waste time with much morality once she accepts you.

Intuitively, I recognized a good many of her qualities instantly. I had no trouble recognizing her beauty. I fell in love with it—and her later.

With whatever urge she took me, I found myself looking in on her that same evening—just to see if she was comfortably situated. That's the story I handed her and myself.

I found her alone and we got talking over a drink she offered me. Next thing you know I had gone out for steaks and was helping her cook dinner. I stayed the entire night. In her bed. By her side. I thought no less of her in the morning in the way of childish regret and condemnation. In fact I was lost from that night on. I found her the embodiment of all the lovers of my dreams. And in a sense, that gave her a dangerous hold on me.

Although I am seventeen years her senior and her popularity would scare off much younger and prettier men, I believe she gave me about as much time as anyone after that amazing first night. The exception might be Doug Coleman who has always been her favorite.

I agree with her choice of Doug. He is one who has grown along the way, hammering experience into the shape of character. He is rich in spirit, he has insight and that selfless quality that makes men great. Yet his weakness lies in his inability to control emotion with an intelligent acceptance of disillusionment. His determination to make Andrea into what he believes she should and could be might easily destroy him—and Andrea, too. He is not a loud noise that will dissipate with the first wind. His power smolders in the lonely hours of brooding contemplation and waits in a basement corner of his soul for combustion. He deserves a proper respect. And a proper fear.

My mind is so full of undigested scraps that I have a distressing tendency to digress. I began to say that Andrea took me into the fold as a sort of mascot and substitute father and then promptly made me her lover. I played many roles for her and enjoyed them all.

I knew pretty quickly that she had an insatiable lust which bordered on what the world, in its hard shell of blind cruelty, would call nymphomania. It's been a long time since anything has come along to shock me, and at first, I stood at a self-protective distance and looked upon her with a faint, cynic-sad amusement.

Then two subtle changes developed in me and

amusement departed, leaving only sadness. Beyond her body and the insidious drug of her love-making and in full recognition of her weaknesses, I fell in love with Andrea as a person. Also, I found that she needed me. Pitifully. Can there be two stronger ties than these?

Fortunately, I did not remind Andrea in any physical or other sense of her father. That would have been the end of our intimacy. No, it would not have begun at all. But I did seem to have the maturity of years and the qualities of a father-substitute for her, while remaining a lover. It put me in a unique position.

Andrea confided, without going into any detail, some of the horror of her childhood. I immediately saw the connection with her present problem. It made everything come clear. She had never had from those two ignorant monsters, her parents, even the most diluted form of real love or affection. She was brought up in a world of cruel animality and grossness. She was never made to feel any more worthy or important than a two dollar prostitute. She never knew the meaning of decent pride or reasonable power. Naturally, she cultivate a whole swarm of crawling inferiorities.

Add to this her exaggerated conception of the importance of money. The lack of money was to her a symbol of near starvation, rags and filth, base toil, insecurity, drunkenness, ignorance, and absolute degradation. On the other hand, the accumulation of money represented to her freedom, power, security, respect, escape, education and the hope of mere childish possession of things. All the bright, shiny things the world thinks will make it happy.

Now. You take this same package of pathetic trouble and insecurity as a scrawny, underdeveloped, ragged little girl and you have nothing but bitter resignation. But give her overnight the body of a highly developed, rarely beautiful woman and she has in her hands a power of which she never dreamed.

And when she finds this power works a marvelous magic, how is she going to use it? Wisely? No! She has no wisdom, only emotional needs and willful drives, self-pity and bitterness. So she takes her power and uses it as a bargaining agent and as a weapon for revenge on a world that scorned her.

She is hungry for this love and affection she has never had. And when she finds that men will give it to her, or an imitation of it (she doesn't know real love) in return for her body, she becomes a glutton, stuffing herself with food that has no nourishment and only leaves her empty. But the emptier she feels, the more she has to feed that need. And so the cycle goes on. That's Andrea. In capsule. Simplified. For there are tides that move us this way and that and they are beyond tracing.

These are the things I told Andrea bit by bit, time by time. And one night she cried and said, "Yes! That's it. I see it. It's all true! Oh, Ralph. My beloved, Ralph. My teacher, my father, my lover. Help me. Save me. From myself. I'm drowning in a loathsome sewer. Don't let me go down, dearest Ralph. Keep talking. Keep protecting. Don't leave me! There is no one else who really understands or cares."

And I said, "I'll always teach you and protect you, poor lost little girl. Because I love you more than myself. And I'll never have to leave you—if you'll marry me. Will you?"

"Yes! Yes, I will, Ralph. I love you, too. And it's the only answer."

"When?"

"I . . . I don't know. I don't know. Give me time. Give me time to think."

So I gave her time and I held her, but not too tightly. I let her go. I didn't insist. I didn't mention her promise. I waited. I watched the eager, possessive lovers come and go, scheming and fighting over her, receiving, most probably, the same promises of marriage. And I strictly forbade myself the luxury of jealousy. I kept it caged outside my thinking like a writhing snake. For I knew it would destroy me.

Meantime she was like a loving, obedient child in

my arms, seeking and giving tenderness while caressing with the body of a woman. Oh, the beauty and the sadness of it, the peace where there was no peace. The restless fever never left her.

How is it you can know causes and still not cure effects? The same old worn and scratchy record spins on and grooves only deeper as though the first sordid impression were the last.

But then, for a space of time, she seemed really to be trying. She made excuses, she broke engagements. She saw no one but me. We made excited plans for marriage. I took her to my home, showed her how we would live—comfortable, secure. We were full of laughter and companionship. She held my hand like a little girl and trusted. Her transformation was the greatest joy of my life. To heal something you love. To save it from self-destruction!

There was a party. One of those Hollywood things that burn with hectic brightness and false gaiety. She was invited by some ad agency executive and took me as her escort. The party is unimportant. Howard Overholtzer was there. He dropped on her like a bomb with all his money and social nothingness and glitter. He was a rather good looking vainglorious dummy. He didn't work. He sat behind a desk and played with toy telephones while staring at a nameplate—President. He wasn't capable of real thought. No one would have given him a second nod. But he sat in his father's chair—when he felt like it—and played the big game. The business was well established. It ran itself. Or was run by competent underlings.

And at that party I lost Andrea. Immediately. Irrevocably. Not that seeing her again was forbidden. Oh, no. The implication was that I would see her often. Later. That I would go right on being her godfather. Because you see, Andrea was the little girl who had gotten her cake. And now she was going to eat it, too.

And so the cycle was completed. Disintegration had fulfilled its destiny.

Right then I tried to put myself aside in order to

take an objective look at Andrea's future. On the surface it looked good. It seemed that she would now have everything that perhaps the world owed her for its abuse. She would certainly have more in material possessions and ease than I could ever offer her. She would also have a man some ten years my junior—if youth alone is an automatic guarantee of happiness.

But after careful probing, I came to the conclusion that this was absolutely the worst thing that could happen to Andrea—especially in the hands of an insensitive like Overholtzer. It might have been different if she really loved this man and if marriage would lock her bedroom door against all but her partner forever.

But I could see that she planned only to indulge herself still further, opening that door still wider and allowing a greater evil to take the place of a lesser. Riches would destroy altogether the little strength that I had been able to give her. Luxury and idleness would bring opportunity for complete abandonment and utter selfishness in debauchery. As alcohol underlines and releases the worst instincts, riches without control of spirit would complete her debasement. All that I had built would crumble. And I wouldn't be able to save her. This was, in disguise as the final crowning, the worst evil that could befall her. It had to be stopped! She needed me!

And then, out of the darkness of a side street, a piece of metal no bigger than the end of your finger, drove through the brain of Howard Overholtzer. The mills of the gods which had ground so slowly had also ground exceedingly fine.

How sad. How cruel. Yet he felt no more than a dart of pain—a bee on the wing, pausing, going away. And the greatest pain is left to the living, a dreadful heritage of sorrows and suffering in a gloomy Fun House of distorted mirrors, hopeless mazes and sealed doors, outside of which a blousy and evil hag, obscenely laughs and laughs and laughs. There is only one exit from this Fun House. And Howard Overholtzer had so unwittingly taken it.

How frail the human shell that so small a piece of metal can end its strutting. All the smugness and the petty power, the social climbing, the pride of possession, the arrogance of position, the conceit of the winner, drained away at the instant of impact. Makes you kind of humble, doesn't it, if you stop to consider?

And, oh, the power, the awful power, loaned to that dark shadow behind the gun. How like some minor god he must feel as his finger slips behind the trigger guard and tightens, tightens; as he looks at the puny and helpless subject under the magnifying glass of his cross-haired, telescopic sight. The decision rests in the muscle of his finger instructed by some secret and dark corner of his brain.

He decides!

The finger squeezes. The figure falls. And the sound of the shot echoes back to him, laughing, laughing, like the blousy Fun House hag.

Andrea Lockridge

I FINALLY REMEMBERED the name of that awful delivery boy. It was Switzer. Willie Switzer. He used to work at that liquor store a few blocks from where Viv and I had an apartment in Glendale. I didn't want to go on living with Viv anyway, but it was really that Willie Switzer who made up my mind in a hurry. I got out of there fast and moved over here in Santa Monica, about as far away as you could get.

Willie used to clerk in the store in the afternoons. Then when the night man came on, he would run orders until about nine or ten. He didn't have a brain in his head, but he was built like Tarzan in a tree. He looked like one of those muscle ads and had hair almost as long as mine. He had a crafty face and dirty eyes. He used to be a lifeguard but if there was one ugly girl on the whole beach, a drowning man wouldn't have a chance.

One thing, I'm sure we got the fastest delivery in town. You would call in an order and while you were hanging up, the door bell would be ringing. If Viv was there, he would give me a fast ogle and leave on the run. But if I was alone, he would hang around talking nonsense until he had stripped me down in his mind like a backyard hot rod.

I hated him. I just hated him! Intellectually, I mean. I treated him like what he was—something that crawled out from under a rock. But he did stir some crazy impulse I don't understand and one night when Viv was out and I had had a fight with Jeff, I sent for a bottle. I was feeling low and restless and mean all at once. I think I knew when I picked up that phone what was going to happen.

After that he was unbearable. Just unbearable! He used to call at all hours and come around unasked even when Jeff or one of my other men friends was there. Imagine! He acted like he owned me. I couldn't explain him and I couldn't get rid of him without calling the police. So I moved.

But today (Wednesday), I did tell the police about him. I simply said that he was no friend of mine and never had been but that he used to hang around and stare like there was something wrong with him upstairs.

That Lieutenant Brehmer said he sounded like the best lead yet. They're out hunting for him now and if they find him I'll deny anything he says about me and be believed. Because it's easy for me to see by the questions I'm asked and the respect with which I'm treated that none of my friends have said an unkind word about me. I choose my men friends carefully and I don't think any of them would betray me. Except for Viv, I leave women out of my life. If you have even a curve you could mark "safe at sixty miles an hour," women will say anything about you.

The newspaper reporters simply will not leave me alone! They keep calling or coming in person and I can't be too rude to them because they can insinuate the foulest things without saying a libelous word. Also they can dig and dig until they do find what they're looking for. So when they come, I offer them a drink —of orangeade—and I'm all sweetness and light. As a result, most of what they say about me reflects a certain sympathy and respect. They finally did get my picture from some model agency file and I must say it was a good one.

But the story is back page news now to everyone but the police who seem relentless in their quiet way. Pressure has been brought to bear in the Overholtzer clan, a reward has been offered, and I'm sure there are police from other precincts out of jurisdiction on the case. It never will rest. And neither will I.

The newspapers have to say something, come up with

some new lead. So now they are harping on the theory that the killer is a madman, some kind of sexual pervert. They back this up with the finally revealed fact that Howie was also shot in the "genitals," as they put it. Disgusting! Every half-baked psychologist who can spell sex deviate has his own pet theory, printed for all to see. Revolting!

Doug came over last night soon after Viv left for the movies. I can see now how foolish I was to worry about him in the least.

He rang the bell and when I answered, he just stood there looking at me with the most compassionate expression I've ever seen on the face of any human being. Honestly, it was almost spiritual. Then he closed the door and he came to me in this slow, tender way, bowing his head over my shoulder and holding me with all his strength and with all his love. But without any passion whatsoever. It was like—well—like Jesus had put his arms around one of his disciples to comfort him after a great sadness. And I don't mean that in any sacreligious way, either. It was one of the most beautiful experiences I have ever known.

Then he sat down with me and held my hand and talked to me very gently, telling me not to be unhappy and not to be afraid because he was always there if I needed him. "Just remember," he said. "This will pass, even this, dear Andrea. And you will have a deeper happiness and a more lasting peace from the experience. Bless suffering if it makes you grow."

Of course I had to go and cry. I'm always crying these days at the least kind thing someone says to me. But after awhile I perked up and mixed a drink which he sipped solemnly and apparently without interest.

Then he told me how sorry he was for all the things he said to me that night at the Ambassador. He said it was the accumulation of his unhappiness at losing me, especially to someone whom he knew would never make me happy. It was the easiest thing in the world to forgive him.

The way he talked I was very quiet inside. For

awhile. And completely without fear of him. Then I began to get this restless ache because I wanted him and he just sat there talking and didn't seem in the least to realize. Finally I had to practically take him by the hand. He said he felt all this love for me and didn't want to dissipate or change it with mere physical passion. Mere physical passion!

Finally he came into the bedroom with me and just laid by my side for the longest time not touching me. But I became a little angry and then he did give in. He made love to me so sweetly, as though some of the old frenzy had gone out of him. It made me love him in a still different way than I have ever known. But I did come away just a trifle unsatisfied. I mean, some part of me. How can there be a mixture of so many things pulling us apart?

When Viv came home, we were sitting across the room from each other as though he had just dropped in for coffee and doughnuts. That kind of tickled me.

I do feel a great deal better than I did a couple of days ago. I have even begun to think of the money I might have had, the glorious freedom from ever wanting again and all the delicious clothes and things in half the shop windows of the world.

Howie's will has been read, though, of course, I wasn't present, and his money seems to have been divided among his relatives who already have plenty. What a waste! And not a mention of me.

Howie was an only child. His parents were divorced about a year before Mr. Overholtzer died. I met his mother, two aunts and an uncle. They were most cordial then, but short and cool when I spoke to them on the phone after Howie was killed. It was as though I was responsible. Imagine! Or were they afraid I might get some of his money?

Anyway, though I feel a little less strained at the surface edge of my nerves, way down below, I am more frightened than ever. They haven't caught him and everything seems to have quieted down. I don't like that. Because in the most ominous way, I feel as though some creeping evil is just waiting to happen.

Jeff called Monday and is coming over tonight. Mark Bristol phoned today for the second time and insists on seeing me. He has been thoroughly questioned by the police and is the first one who seems willing to tell me more than just a few general facts. Why the others are kind of silent makes me wonder.

Mark is just a couple of years older than I am. He is strangely grown up and childish at the same time. He is a very sensitive type. Much too sensitive, I think, sometimes. He is six feet three or four, I forget. About the tallest man I know. He is rather slim, which adds to the impression of height. He is very nice looking, though not in the powerful way of men like Doug and Jeff. He has this pale, aesthetic looking face and hair about the color of cinnamon. He wears octagonal glasses that seem to melt into his personality so that you never notice them. Sometimes he has the studious and distracted air of a movie type college professor. Typical, I mean. He is in love with me in this terribly serious way, sometimes to the extent that it becomes dull. He has the most artistic, long-fingered hands I've ever seen. To look at him you would never think where those hands have been and how clever they are—with a woman.

I really don't want to see him, or Jeff, either, for that matter. Now, I mean. Everyone scares me but Doug and maybe Ralph Whiting. But imagine my predicament. Now that Howie is gone, God save him, they all want to see me. Every one. Let's say I refuse to see them. And then suppose that one of them did this terrible thing out of some insane jealousy or twisted hate. Well, can you imagine his reaction? He has killed Howie and now he is still thwarted. That diseased brain of his begins to boil again. Wouldn't he come and kill me next or say Doug, coming out of my apartment some night? He just might. I think he would. I'm almost sure of it. Because whatever his plan, it would still be incomplete without me.

I almost wish it was that Willie Switzer who did it. He seems far more dangerous and evil than the others. But obviously so. Somehow you feel you could cope with him. But the others are subtle. You could look into their faces and never know what was going on behind their eyes. Therefore, in that way, they seem far more dangerous.

So you understand, I have to see them all. I must be almost subservient to them. I must be very cautious. I must watch their every expression and change. I must do or say nothing to displease the least of them. One word, one wrong step would be like lighting a fuse. And I don't want to die. I don't ever, ever want to die!

My God, if there is a God. If you are there. Save me. Or at least tell me . . .

Which one? Which one!

William Switzer

THIS ANDREA is a babe you don't forget. Once you get so much as a peep at her, you couldn't wipe her out of your mind if you fell two stories on your head. And I got more than a peep. I got a hell of a good look. Fact, I had her when she was good!

I come up to her apartment one night with some booze. That was when I was workin' in this package store in Glendale. I only caught her alone twice—the first time and the last time. Jesus! That last time!

But this first time I won't forget neither. She come to the door in this filmy, black lace thing. Maybe it was pink. What's the difference? It didn't hide nothing. And she had more than enough for one guy. She was built when bricks were cheap! She could of thrown away half her curves and had enough left over to build a roller coaster.

I got one look at her and goddamned near dropped the bottle. But I played dumb. I asked her if I could use her phone to check back with the store. I just wanted to stall. She give me a look about ten below but she let me in and showed me where it was. The phone.

I dialed with the receiver down and held a nice long conversation with myself. Meantime, I let my globes wander around the place, checking to see if maybe there was some sign she had a husband. This place had a very female type look, a lot of frills. I figured her for a loner.

Meantime, she walks by a couple of times. I study her like she was a problem in geometry with all them crazy angles. I had a hard time talkin' because I was slobberin' all over myself.

87

Finally I had to quit. I hung up. I just run out of words. Then I went back in the living room where she was sittin' in a chair havin' a cool one. I says to her, "Listen, you mind if I wait around for a few minutes? I'm expecting a call from the store. They got another place they may want to send me. I give them this number."

She gives me this kind of careful, kind of snooty look made you want to slap her in the puss. "You should have asked me before you give them the number," she says. "Seems to me you take a lot for granted. But now that you done it, you kin wait."

She didn't ask me to sit down or nothing. But I did anyway. We just stared at each other. At least I stared at her. And the things I was thinkin' you wouldn't see in one of them dirty comic books I got in my room.

I asked her a lot of questions about if she lived alone and what she did for a living. Things like that. She mostly said nothin' or give me short answers. Finally I got sick of it, so I said, "Well, guess they ain't gonna call. I'll run on back there." Then I left. But I never got her outta my kind.

Next time we got a call from her I beat it over there fast. But this time she had some other babe with her. Roommate, I guess. The other one was just the opposite. She did things to me about like one of them cigar store Indians. So I left without no foolin' around. I just give her a look that told her I knew where she kept everything she got and what it was.

She made me mad because she was the first babe in my life I couldn't make——like that! Just like that! She just kept stirrin' around in my mind until I owed her a boodle just for what I thought.

Then one night she calls and I go up there and this time she's alone. She greets me a little different. I don't know how to explain it. Just different. Maybe she smiled a little or somethin'. Anyway I got the feeling, so I walk right in and ask her if she would like me to put the ginger ale I picked up for her at another store in the refrigerator. She said that would be very nice. Then she paid me and it was the first time she didn't give me a tip. That was some kind of cue right there.

She was wearin' this same flimsy outfit but pulled a little more away from her shoulders. I knew from the beginning there was something there for the right guy. I was it, but before it hadn't been the right time. Know what I mean?

After she give me the money, I just stood there lookin' her over. I asked her if she don't get lonely sometimes with no man around. She said, "Sure, but what are you gonna do? I'm new in Glendale and I don't know no one." I knew this was a lie because she would have an army following her like Joan of Arc if she even walked down the street.

So I said, "Well, now you know me!"

She didn't say nothin', but she give me this funny smile and I saw her swallow once or twice like her throat was dry. I just walked right up to her and put my arms around her like I had been doin' that for years with her.

She pulled away a little. They all have to do that, make it look good. Then she just fell against me and opened her lips, big, wide ones like feather pillows, and I almost fell in her mouth. Then she pushed me away and went around puttin' out all the lights but one and bringin' down the shades.

I come into the living room where she was standing by the light. She smiles like a cat that wanted to eat the canary and hooks her thumbs in this flimsy thing she was wearin' and pulls it right open and lets it drop to the floor.

So help me, she was wild naked!

"How do you like me?" she says. Just like that.

Well, my God! Good Christ! I couldn't even talk. You never saw such a body in your whole life. They just can't make 'em that way no more. It was enough to make you tremble all over.

I finally got my wits and took her into the bedroom. Christ almighty! If she wasn't the best I ever had in my life! She turned me every way but loose. And she was no bum. She got to me. I would have mopped her floors just to be around her. Just to have her once more. But I never did. Never again. And not because I didn't try!

Afterwards she began to cry and mumble about being ashamed and all that. Then she seemed to get crazy mad at me but it was really herself she was mad at. She didn't want to do it but she couldn't resist me.

She kicked me right out and told me not to come back. I just laughed at her.

I come back all the time after that. She never would see me. Never called for booze no more. Seems like every time I come over, there was some classy lookin' guy sittin' around. Made me mad. She thought she was too good for me. I could of killed her. Givin' it to the big shots—everyone but me.

I used to call her in the middle of the night, lyin' on my bed. I used to remind her about that time. And I used to tell her what I was goin' to do with her next time I seen her. Things she maybe never heard of before.

But after a couple of times like that, she hung up right away when she heard who it was.

Then she moved and I didn't see her again for about a year or more. Never stopped thinkin' about her meantime. Drove me crazy. Hated her and loved her at the same time. Wanted to kill her and love her all at once. Wanted to beat the brains out of every one of them slick boy friends. Dudes!

Then one day I was down at the beach in Santa Monica. Used to be a lifeguard out that way. Saw her on the beach. Big as life and twice as sexy.

I didn't let on I seen her. She didn't get a peek at me either. But I followed her home, found out where she lived. I knew she wouldn't have nothin' to do with me, so I didn't ring her bell.

But after that I used to sneak around at night and look in her window. There was this balcony led around in back of her apartment and went right by her bedroom window. This window had some kind of folding blind. But the goddamn thing hung loose and if you peeked in at the side, you could pretty near see the whole crazy room. You could watch her undress. Jesus! What a sight! It used to knock somethin' loose in my head.

Sometimes I would watch guys in that bedroom, too. Christ! You can't stand much of that.

Finally, I read where she was gonna get married to this millionaire playboy. I recognized this guy from his picture. I hated that sonofabitch worse than the others because he was gonna take her right outta circulation. I wouldn't never be able to get to her or watch no more. And, by then, watchin' was like I caught some itch I couldn't never scratch away. It got so I wanted that more than her. It was crazy. But I had to have it!

Then this here guy got shot in the head one night right outside her place. I was so happy I wanted to send flowers. Now I could go right back to that window again. I was just about married to that goddamned window anyway. And them cops is gone now.

I'm goin' over there tonight!

Mark Bristol

TWO PLAINCLOTHES POLICEMEN came to my office on Flower Street in Los Angeles. That was Tuesday. A couple of days ago. I'm research director for West Coast Oil and fortunately I have my own private office. I wouldn't have wanted anyone to hear the sort of questions these men asked.

One of the officers was a Lieutenant Brehmer and the other's name was Kauffman, I believe. I know they have a job to do and I suppose they were friendly enough under the circumstances. But I don't think it was necessary to humiliate me with the most intimate type of questions about my relationship with Andrea. I realize there is a gruesome murder involved, but I don't know why it is the police think every man and woman in the world keep company on a purely sensual basis of the lowest order. Of course they are used to dealing with the very dregs and have no sensitivity where normal and respectable citizens are concerned.

The one called Brehmer seemed to have the most to say. He spoke so softly that I could hardly hear him. Sometimes I had to ask him what he had said. But I watched his face, and especially his eyes, closely. It seemed to me that withal there was something a little patronizing in his manner. I felt a small current of resentment at this. But I was too frightened and ill at ease to let it show. I have never been comfortable around law officials of any kind and I feel a little panicky even when confronted by something like a traffic violation.

After Brehmer and Kauffman entered my office, they made an attempt at cordiality that fell about as flat as a pointless joke. They sat down and Brehmer began the questioning. At first it was just routine— Where do you live? What are your duties with West Coast Oil and how long have you been in their employ, age, marital status and so on. Then there was a silence while Brehmer offered me a cigarette. I refused and he lighted one himself, staring out the window, then turning back, looking down, then up sharply into my eyes.

"Have you ever been arrested for a felony?" he said.

I don't know why, but the question startled me. "I'm afraid I don't know exactly what you mean," I said. "I'm not too well versed in legal terminology."

"I mean a crime or offense of a serious nature— robbery, arson, rape, murder."

"Heavens, no!" I said. "Nothing more serious than a traffic violation."

He nodded absently and seemed to lose interest in the question.

"How did you meet Miss Andrea Lockridge?"

"I met her at a beach club dance. I was introduced to her."

"How long have you known her?"

"A little over a year now."

"And how would you define your relationship with her? Are you close? Or are you just casual friends?"

"Oh, no. We are very close. In an unofficial way, you might say we are engaged."

"How can that be if Miss Lockridge was to marry the deceased, Howard Overholtzer?"

"Well, what I mean to say is that before that we . . ."

"In other words, your engagement or understanding was broken off when Miss Lockridge announced her intention to marry Overholtzer."

"Yes."

The two men exchanged brief glances. Kauffman spoke.

"Mr. Bristol, didn't this break anger you or at least cause resentment?"

I was well awere of what he was driving at. "No

sir," I said. "Not resentment or anger. You might say I was troubled. Upset. Extremely disappointed."

Kauffman leaned back, apparently satisfied. Brehmer spoke again.

"Did you approve of Mr. Overholtzer?"

"I neither approved nor disapproved of him. I wanted Andrea to be happy."

"You had no feelings about him whatsoever?"

The truth was that I despised him. He was full of stupid conceit and he was completely unworthy of her. "Well," I said, "I was not well enough acquainted with him to judge him." I knew him quite well through Andrea and meetings at various parties. "He wasn't anyone I would have made a second choice for Andrea. But, of course, the decision wasn't mine and I suppose one rival is as bad as another."

"Oh? Then he was a rival? You felt that?"

"I believe I had a normal reaction to being deprived of something so precious to me. I was emotionally upset."

"So then you took action to prevent it," Kauffman said.

"No, sir," I said. "I did nothing." Kauffman was too obvious to upset me. Brehmer continued, fingering the brim of his hat, allowing his gaze to drift upward from a point on my chest to my eyes.

"When did you first have sexual intercourse with Miss Lockridge?"

"What's that?"

"I said, when did you first have sexual intercourse with Miss Lockridge?"

"Why, I . . . It was . . . I never did! I never did such a thing. She wouldn't have allowed it and I wouldn't have . . . Anyway, I don't see what bearing . . ."

"You mean to tell me, Mr. Bristol, that you were practically engaged to this beautiful girl that any man would give his right arm to sleep with and you never laid a hand on her? Come now. There are no ladies present, we are all men—I hope. Let's talk like men!"

I could have jabbed an ice pick in his throat and watched him bleed. Beautiful, sweet Andrea. My darling. "I know how it may seem to you, lieutenant, with the type of people you run across in your work. But I think anyone will tell you Miss Lockridge's morals are beyond reproach. Our relationship was on a strictly high level."

The two officers exchanged rather smug glances. Brehmer said, "I'm getting pretty sick of hearing that crap from all you silk handkerchief boys. You can't all be fairies. And you'd have to be. You mean to say you never so much as played handsies with her?"

"I resent your tone and the entire line of questioning you're taking, lieutenant," I said finally.

"In case you don't know it, Mr. Bristol, voluntary sex is no crime in this state. Murder is! We are through pussy-footing around with you choir boys. We want the whole dirty truth and we intend to get it. This man Overholtzer was shot and the murderer was one hell of a good shot. He knew what he was shooting at."

There is nothing you can say to a man like Brehmer. I remained silent.

He sat there staring at me, his face suddenly closed. He spoke softly again.

"How is it that all of you men were engaged to Miss Lockridge without benefit of ring and each one of you thought she was going to marry you? Was this a kind of club? Were you going to have a group marriage?"

I could feel the color mounting to my face. My ears burned. "Aside from myself and Howard Overholtzer, Mis Lockridge had no plans to marry anyone."

"If you had an agreement to marry her, how come she was seeing a half dozen others at the same time?"

"Well, since we weren't—since we hadn't announced our engagement, I felt she should be perfectly free to go out. I encouraged her. I wanted her to be sure."
Actually I had begged her practically on my knees to

give up the others. But she wouldn't hear of it. We fought about it all the time. But you can't tell that to a man like Brehmer. The best way to deal with a brute instinct is to keep your mouth shut and your feelings to yourself.

Brehmer stood up and his stooge did likewise. Brehmer reached out his hand and I took it reluctantly. He was smiling broadly.

"No hard feelings," he said. "We have to get the job done or this town wouldn't be safe to live in." He looked around the office. "Pretty nice setup you have here. Like your work?" His whole manner was friendly now and I found myself thawing a little. I am quick to forgive people when they show a little decency.

"Yes," I said. "I like it very much here."

"I suppose there isn't a job in the world doesn't bore hell out of you now and then. People think we have a time," he said confidentially. "But it's about one-tenth excitement and nine-tenths routine."

I smiled pleasantly. "Guess that's right," I said. "Nothing is the way it seems from the outside."

"You've got to have hobbies," he said with a wink. "I do a lot of fishing. And hunting, too. You like hunting? We could get together sometime."

"Well, sure," I said, beginning to like him. "But it's been a long time. I've about forgotten how."

"You like to hunt deer?"

"Used to."

"That's my specialty. You take that Winchester .30-06 with a telescopic sight and you've got a sweet gun for deer-hunting. Why with a gun like that a good shot could drill a fifty cent piece at a hundred, even a hundred and fifty yards. Don't you think that's the best gun?"

"Well, yes, I suppose . . ."

"Isn't that what you use?"

"Well, no. I . . ."

"Where do you keep your guns? Isn't that stupid! At home, naturally."

I guess I had known in the back of my mind all

along what he was driving at. But he was so friendly. I hated him more than before. Much more. A sly, sneaky animal.

"I don't have any guns, lieutenant. I haven't had one for years."

His smile flickered and went out. "How come we found a rifle just like that and traced it to you?"

We stared across the desk at each other. Even then I had a quick stab of doubt. His expression was so positive. "It was a good try, lieutenant," I said. "But now if you have no more questions, I have work to do."

He had been leaning toward me. He straightened up and put his hat carefully on his head. I was faintly amused to learn that detectives do take their hats off. Not just when they're climbing under a shower.

"I would advise you to keep this conversation to yourself, Mr. Bristol. There are still people we could catch by surprise and I'm sure you want this murder solved. I would be especially careful to say nothing to Miss Lockridge since she is in contact with the others and since there are certain subjects that might prove embarrassing to her. We don't want to hurt anyone. We just want the truth. There is only one person going to get hurt in this thing."

Again my contempt for him wavered. "You can be sure I'll have nothing to say to anyone."

"And, Mr. Bristol, if for any reason you find it necessary to leave town for more than a day, please call me at this number." He handed me a card. "If you remember anything or dig up anything that might be of help, get right in touch. Good-bye, sir." They left.

I picked up the phone and called Andrea.

She seemed in better spirits than she had the last time I talked to her. I told her that I had just been cross-examined by Brehmer and Kauffman. She wanted to know what it was all about and I said, "I'll tell you when I come over Thursday evening. They don't want you to know anything about what line they're following, but I think for your protection you should. You do want to see me, don't you?"

"Well, I . . . Of course, I do, Mark! It seems like just ages."

I didn't like the way she hesitated there for just a second. Had she lost interest in me? "You still do care about me, don't you, Andrea?"

"Oh, yes, Mark. You know I do."

"You never were really in love with Howard?"

"Not really, Mark. Not really. I just thought so."

"Then you . . . you are in love with me?"

Silence. Then, "Yes, you should know that I . . ."

"Why did you hesitate?"

"Mark. Mark! Please stop it. Don't you know that I've been through a terrible experience and I'm pulled every which way and I can't even think. Besides, I don't want to talk of personal things on the phone."

"I'm sorry. Is Viv going to be home tomorrow evening?"

"I don't know. I'll see what I can do. But I can't just shove her out every night. She's been an angel."

"Come over to my place. Ted has a meeting. Republican Club."

"I'm frightened to go anywhere, Mark. Sometimes I wonder if I'll ever leave here until they find him."

"I understand. Around eight then? Tomorrow night."

"Around eight. Bye."

I hung up with a feeling of utter depression. I'm sure Andrea is beginning to cool as far as I'm concerned. Those little hesitations . . . Or could it be that I'm mistaking fear for lack of interest? Andrea says I'm too sensitive. And maybe she's right. But most people bull through life knocking over your feelings like so many tin cans in an alley.

Sometimes I will go down the hall and I will pass one of the vice-presidents or Hardesty, the sales manager, or sometimes just some little secretary. And I will give them a big hello and they will pass right by me like they were sleep-walking or something. Or they will merely grunt, which is just as bad. No manners! Not even common courtesy. Arrogant pigs!

And I will think, what have I done? Or not done?

Or said? I'm the head of a department. Don't I deserve a certain respect? Is it because I'm young for such responsibility? Is it jealousy? It spoils a whole day for me just wondering.

Then next time I meet the same person, he might fairly beam all over me. And that makes my day. For awhile I feel important and needed. Sometimes I feel so elated and other times I feel tears crowding behind my eyes. Like when Brehmer dropped that soft pose and spoke to me in that harsh, menacing way, leaning forward with his chin thrust out, his eyes cold with contempt and smug power.

My father used to talk to me that way when I was a kid and didn't live up to some expectation of his, usually in athletics. He wanted me always to be a winner, especially in a physical way. I was terribly afraid of him and I used to try. But I never could win at anything outside the mental realm.

He used to say, "Look at you. Just look at the size of you! And you couldn't lick your sister with one hand tied behind your back. Go on! Go on and play with your dolls."

From then on I always hated brute force. And power. And authority. I always liked women. They seemed so soft. And tender. Certain men, like Brehmer, I have always despised. And avoided. And secretly wanted to crush. Because I was afraid of them. I read once that all our acts are acts of fear. And it's true.

Sometimes I will be walking down the street, or just sitting in my office, or coming up the stairs to my place, getting out my keys, and all of a sudden, for no reason, I will have this slow, crawling sensation of fear. And not even know what I'm afraid of. It might go back to the time when as a boy I would come home around supper time and stand a long while outside the front door until I got up courage enough to go in. I was afraid. Because I didn't know what my father was going to do or say next.

Or it could be just a nameless fear that comes out of the atmosphere. From nowhere. Because my father is old now and I see that he was only a bully. Like Brehmer.

But why should I be afraid of Brehmer? What can he possibly know about me?

One thing did bother me and that was why he didn't ask where I was at the time of the murder. You would think they would always ask that first. It bothered me a lot. It made me very uneasy. But then I found out that soon after he left me, he went over and had a talk with Ted Rolley who shares an apartment with me. Ted told me.

Ted said Brehmer asked if Ted knew what I was doing Saturday night. And Ted said he answered that he knew very well because he was with me. We had dinner out and went to a picture and got back around ten. We talked for a little while and then went to bed.

Brehmer wanted to know how Ted could be sure I didn't go out after he fell asleep. And Ted said he knew because he got up to go to the bathroom around three in the morning and I was sound asleep. That satisfied Brehmer because the murder took place at three.

But Ted told me that he never got up to go to the bathroom at all. And I know he's such a sound sleeper you could hold a party and he wouldn't hear it. So I asked him why he said that. He told me, "I knew you didn't do it. You're just not the type, old buddy. But I also knew that if you didn't have a sound alibi, Brehmer was the sort who would never leave you alone. So I figured I'd get him off your neck."

That's why I share a place with a guy like Ted. Oh yes, and also Brehmer asked if he could look around and Ted let him because it would look bad for me if he didn't. Of course, Brehmer and his stooge didn't find anything.

I had never been in love before I met Andrea. That is, not in any serious way. You hear about people who just look at someone and suddenly they're in love in that dreamy, almost mindless way. And you think it's just the kind of stuff they make songs and

stories of. But it happened just that way with me.
I took one look at her and I felt almost faint. It was
like there was an undeveloped negative in my mind,
I saw her across the room and the sight of her poured
a chemical over my brain—and there she was—printed!
And after that, nothing anyone in the world could
do or say would destroy the print.

That was the beginning of a kind of half ecstacy and
half pain I've never known. Ecstacy when I could
look at her or touch her and when we made love
in that wild or sometimes sinuous and hypnotic way,
a need from which there is no escape except in death.
Or pain when we would argue or especially when she
was with somone else seen or unseen.

I couldn't bear to see anyone touch her even as you
must in dancing or the simple act of being guided
across the street. I would turn away on the edge of
tears if for instance in dancing, she would look up
into another man's face and smile or laugh with their
faces so close together.

I could never understand why, if she loved me as
she said she did, if she planned some day to marry me,
why she had to go out with five or six different men,
seeing me only once a week. She would say that I
should give her every chance to be sure. Or she
would say that she had so many friends before she
met me and she couldn't just cut them off until
she had made up her mind that the time had come to
marry me. Or she would say that she just wanted to
have her "fling" (a word that made me cringe)
before she settled down.

None of these reasons ever convinced me or put
me at ease. The only time I ever knew any peace from
jealousy so intense it was like physical pain was
during that torpid interval of about five or ten minutes
after we made love.

I used to plead and beg her to marry me instantly.
Instantly! And give up these other men forever. And
when she refused or put me off in that rather jocular
and teasing manner, the torture of it would well up

inside me and I would put my head in her lap and weep uncontrollably.

At first she was tender, said comforting words and stroked my head. Then when it had happened several times she would grow angry with me and speak sharply in a cold command to stop it. Once she even said in the most sarcastic and bored tone, "What, again?" Whereupon I lifted my head and slapped her across the face.

I didn't mean it. I was humiliated. My pride was shattered. I'm always striking back in a blood-red blindness when someone destroys my last grain of self-respect. And then immediately feeling morbidly sorry and finally quite normal again.

We had a terrible scene after that slap, with her calling me a cry baby, a mamma's boy and other such verbal knife thrusting. But finally each forgave the other and what followed was the most thrilling and exhausting passion in which we forgave also with our bodies.

I think from that night on, I was hopelessly her slave.

But when I knew she was out with perhaps Doug or Jeff or one of the others, I would walk for hours, not knowing where I was going. It could rain and I wouldn't notice it. And I would have these unforgivably evil pictures of what they were doing, though I knew she was incapable of such faithlessness and impurity. But still I made up stories of where she was at that moment and what she was doing—now dancing, now holding hands beneath a table, now parked on a lonely road, her clothes disarrayed, breath coming in short gasps, now behind the locked door of her apartment, slowly removing the last of her underthings and standing naked before some faceless man who watched and watched and watched . . .

There was the most terrible torture in these picture stories. Yet, if in some searchless perversity one can nurture his pain, I also did that. In the strangest way I cherished my pictures, wouldn't let them go and found in them a twisting undercurrent of excitement.

It was on a Sunday over a week ago that she told me about Howard Overholtzer. They had been seeing each other for a month or so off and on, but aside from the fact that he was immensely rich and wealth is always a silent threat, I paid no more attention to him than the others. He was just another thorn. I don't think I liked him any more or less because, automatically, I hated them all.

But on this Sunday I called her and after some hesitation and fencing around, she told me that she was going to marry Overholtzer in two weeks to the day and that she would be unable to see me again.

I was unable to speak for something like a minute, staring at the receiver in my hand as though it were some kind of reptile that had just bitten me. There followed ten or fifteen minutes of what I will call conversation for lack of a better name. From my end, it was more like hysterics. I heard the sound of my own voice between sobs and was confused as to whether the pleading came from Andrea or myself, since both voices had a decidedly high pitched and feminine quality.

I remember that she was assuring me that it was not over, that she would see me again after they came back from Europe and we would be as close as ever. That was such nonsense that I thought she was merely placating me with the first inanity that came into her head and paid no attention to it whatsoever.

Finally when I stopped choking and shouting and crying all at once, this cold, unmerciful calm swept over me. And I said, "Andrea? Andrea? Are you there?"

But the phone was dead.

It is, of course, a frightful thing that Howard Overholtzer became as dead as that phone in my hand not a week later. After my first uncontrollable joy, I was terribly, terribly, even morbidly, sorry. Death is a black horror beyond understanding. Death cuts the connection forever. There are no phones. No calls can ever reach you; no mail, no shout or plea, no silly spirit messages.

The last hands to touch you with their antiseptic whiteness and their impersonal groping, their trocar probing incision and draining, are those of the embalmer, the mortician and his assistant. Other hands, those gentle, female hands, would recoil with loathing at the thought of ever touching you again.

I often wonder about death and I am beside myself with fear. It is the fear from which all fear springs. I am in mortal terror of tight, smothering places and the grave is a claustrophobic horror beyond imagining. I can only hope for myself and those like poor Howard who have departed, that after death there is no stealthy awakening of the mind to its breathless confinement, while the body, which must never have been empowered with self-awareness, slowly crumbles away.

And if I must go, let it never be with a bullet crashing through my head and gouging my eye, delaying for the merest fraction of a second, just long enough to lay open my features with its soft-nosed spreading, then whining away, as though even now disappointed.

Yes, that was a sickening way for Howard to go and I feel terribly, terribly sorry for him. I'm going to tell Andrea just how sorry when I see her.

Tomorrow!

Andrea Lockridge

THE POLICE have discovered that Willie Switzer, that long-haired monster, has a record. He went to reform school for attempted rape when he was younger and a couple of years ago was arrested for exposing himself in front of high school girls. Later he was released. They are always releasing these sex perverts from one kind of institution or another as perfectly fine. Just fine! Only to have them rape or murder someone a couple of weeks later.

Anyway, the police are now convinced that Willie is the murderer. However, he quit his job at that liquor store and moved away without leaving a clue as to where he might be going. The police are frantically searching for him but have kept the information from the newspapers. This I found out from Lieutenant Brehmer this morning, Friday.

My reaction has been a mixture of relief, confusion and fear. I am relieved to think that perhaps none of my friends were involved in the murder. I'm confused because in a way I find it impossible to believe that Willie is the type to hide in the dark with a high-powered rifle and kill because of some lewd and unsatisfied desire, or some warped pride at being refused. Yet there are lesser and far stranger motives on record. So, I'm confused. And I'm frightened because they haven't found him and if he was the killer he may still be wandering around the neighborhood.

I asked Lieutenant Brehmer why he doesn't put a man here again on guard duty. He told me that a uniformed officer would scare Willie away if he is around. And I said, could anything be better? And he said they don't want to scare him away, they want to catch him, that I'm perfectly safe if I remain inside at night.

What they are going to do is to have a patrol car cruising around the neighborhood at night, making a periodic check of my street and the one from which the shot came.

Well, I don't know. It might work and it might not. I read in the paper that the killer who shot Howie didn't leave a single clue except those mashed .30-06 bullets and the shells from which they were fired. So it seems to me that a person as clever as that would find a way to kill me in spite of any little patrol car checking every half hour or so. I have this awful conviction that if anyone wants to kill you badly enough and they have half a brain, they will find a method to do it.

Yet the murderer didn't intend to kill me originally or he would have with the second shot. The police say the shots were fired by an expert marksman who knew exactly what he was doing and probably used a Winchester with a telescopic sight. I read that in the paper Monday, two days after it happened. So if he didn't intend to kill me then, why now?

I have been especially careful not to offend a single man I know—just in case. I've had to pledge my undying love to each one of them and a promise to marry. Of course, Ralph Whiting and Bud Masterson I've only talked to on the phone. Ralph will be over tonight (Friday) and Bud on Saturday. Then I will have seen them all.

Bud Masterson is a former football star and looks it. He played half-back for U.C.L.A. He is the kind that will be fat in a few years if he doesn't watch himself. He's one big hunk of man, rippling with brawn. You don't notice it so much when he's fully dressed, but . . . Anyway, he's not disgustingly muscle bound or anything like that.

He's blonde and has those big, rugged, all-American features that tighten up and would scare you half to death if you were across the line from him on the opposing team. But he speaks very softly and has a rather quiet and gentle manner—at times. Other times he's full of the devil in a reckless, who-cares, let's-really-live manner.

He's the best physical specimen in the body that I know. And perhaps the worst in the face. I mean his features are too irregular to call him handsome. He looks like a big boulder fell off a cliff and broke just that way—his features, I mean.

Contrary to public opinion, not all football players are dopes. Bud was always in the top bracket of his class. And I put him right up there with Doug and Ralph for sensitivity and understanding. Only he doesn't take life so seriously. He just laughs and squeezes every drop out of living. I have a special love for that big boy. But there are sides of him that I don't think he reveals to anyone. Those are the sides, the hidden ones, I wonder about.

I've been seeing each one in the order they called. I didn't want to show any preference or appear to play favorites. Imagine! I don't even have free will any more. Honestly, I'm so afraid. During the first ten minutes when they come into the room I keep studying their faces, trying to see if there is anything hidden or dangerous in the least expression or glance. At first each face seems foreign to me and somehow dark and threatening. It is as though years had gone by and I am meeting a stranger who has undergone all the subtle changes that years can bring. And then suddenly we reach some familiar ground, some remembered incident or remark typical of that person, and everything is all right again.

I saw Jeff Wednesday and Mark last night. I had a simply wild reunion with Jeff and had no trouble convincing him that Howie was just a form of temporary insanity and that after a decent interval, we can go on with our old plans for marriage. Actually, if I could get Doug off my mind, Jeff would be my second choice because we are very compatible. Very!

And while Jeff is not wealthy, he could buy and sell the others. He's such an egotist, he's already sure of me.

I had a more difficult time with Mark because even when I'm under the spell with him, so to speak, I'm unable to sound completely sincere. I say the right things but they come out forced. There's some weakness in Mark that is almost effeminate at times. Also, he is so pleadingly in love with me that I find him rather a bore.

This is bad because he is so sensitive. And so sorry for himself. The least little thing you say or don't say, he picks right up and makes something of it. It builds and builds until he gets practically hysterical. He has no confidence and his jealousy would scare you to death. In order to get rid of him last night I had to promise that after this week I would see no one but him. A promise I can't possibly keep. And what if he's the one! He could be. Of them all, I'm beginning to wonder most about him.

Honestly, this is the most awful mess. I feel trapped. Each day another rope tightens around me. I've made so many promises I don't remember what they were or to whom they were given. Luckily I never set a precedent by going steady with anyone but Howie. Otherwise I'd be in a hopeless jam.

And all this time, Viv has been a problem, too. She says the most wonderfully kind and flattering things to me, smiling in all the right places and helping me with strategy as though she were my chief of staff. But sometimes I sneak a look at her when she's unaware and see that she is not happy at all. Her eyes get kind of glazed as though she were looking inward at this terribly deep sullenness and brooding.

Last night I told her, "You know, Viv, when all the shouting dies down, I have a pretty good idea what's going to happen."

She looked up, startled. "What's that?"

"I'm going to marry Doug. He's the only one I really love and therefore he's the only one who can keep me from hurting myself any further. I don't know, this awful business of poor Howie has kind of jolted me into a little sense. If I'm going to have to settle for less, I'm going to settle for Doug. I'd be miserable without him."

"Never!" she practically shouted. "You'll never be happy with just one man in your whole life." Then she smiled. "Of course, I do think Doug is an angel. But please don't try to kid yourself, Andrea dear," (I've finally got her to calling me Andrea), "you'll only be asking for more trouble. If I were you, I'd get rid of them all. Just disappear for awhile and start all over again. We could go back to Buffalo for a few months. I could take a leave of absence, or just quit. There are plenty of jobs. I mean, Andrea, after all! You've caused one murder and maybe another is festering right now. You can't toy with people's emotions and expect them to come up with flowers—unless they're lilies. And honey, baby, the way things are going, those lilies might be for you."

I was so horrified I couldn't speak. And then before I began to cry, I did gasp, "Viv! How could you? What a thing to say!"

She obviously hadn't meant it because she put her arm around me and let me cry on her shoulder. "I'm sorry, sweetie," she said. "Terribly sorry. It's just that I stand by watching and see you headed right over the cliff and can't stop it. I can't protect my baby. You've been dealing the cards from the bottom for so long, you don't realize you can get caught. It's not a game for little girls. But you marry Doug or anyone you want to, dear, and I'll stand by you. Just tell Doug to carry a gun and keep looking over his shoulder. Oh, there I go. I'm just kidding and it really isn't so bad. Just please be careful!"

Well, no matter what she said, after that I didn't feel any better. Because I knew she was right. I told her I was all the more convinced that I should marry Doug, even for my own safety. He's so strong and steady! She said, well, maybe that would be for the best.

Meantime I feel compelled, in more ways than one, to see all my men friends at least once more. After all, I am in the best position to find out what's going on in their minds. But we have to be alone and there is always the problem of Viv. I don't ask her to go to the movies. I just tell her someone is coming and she offers with that attitude of weary resignation.

Of course she doesn't always go to the movies. Sometimes she comes home just reeking of whiskey and I know she's been sitting at some local bar. She's so pathetic! At first, when I was under such a strain, I thought it would all work out fine—having her around. But now she shows no sign of leaving. She has this strong, protective instinct and attachment and I don't know how to get rid of her. I'll have to tell her soon and then there'll be a scene. Dear God, could anyone be more hopelessly involved than I am?

There is this business of money to think about. What a nuisance! I took the engagement ring to one place for appraisal and sold it at another. It was appraised at about twenty-seven thousand. Disappointing! But worse, it sold for only twelve thousand five hundred. Imagine! It's just like stealing. They stole it from me. Still—I can get by for a year or more without working if I have to. But I can't stand another week of this. I'm going to marry Doug! Then later, maybe . . . Oh, I don't know!

The most shocking thing happened last night after Mark left. I was terrified. It was before Viv came home and I was alone. I was sitting in the dark, looking out the window. I was smoking a cigarette and watching for Viv. I always sit in the dark and watch for her because I don't like to just hear someone come in. I want to know who it is. And sometimes, if Viv is a little tight, she will ring the bell and I won't answer unless I know it's she.

Anyway, there I was watching. There is this balcony that goes around my apartment, right past my windows. And all of a sudden, this shadow went slinking by right in front of me. I couldn't see who it was—but it was a man!

I began to shake all over the way I did the night Howie was killed. I ran to the phone and called the police. For once it only took them about three minutes—plenty of time for me to have been murdered.

But when they did come, there wasn't a sign of anyone and they told me I was still suffering from nerves; speaking in that half serious manner as though to a child coming up out of a dark basement. So I made coffee and before they had finished, Viv came home.

I pretended to believe that I had been suffering hallucinations. What can you do? But that was a man! A very big man. It could have been almost any one of them. And he'll probably be back!

I know the end is in sight now and I'm scared—like someone waiting to be executed. Because I know I have done great harm to some people, however unwittingly. And maybe there is a God or just some force that punishes. Some force that sends someone or something out of the night to carry out my sentence. But if I must pay some awful penalty—then hurry!

Because I am slowly strangling with fear.

Bud Masterson

MY GOD! Old Howie Overholtzer got shot right in the bean and also where his brains were. Poor bastard. Well now look, Howie—it can't get much worse! That's the beauty of it. It can't get much worse. When they've taken that, they've got it all and they leave you alone.

Well, if he had to go, and we all do, he sure left a nice inheritance. And I don't mean his dough, I mean Andrea, they-threw-the-mold-away, Lockridge.

Andrea is quite a gal. Crazy. Mixed up like an old-fashioned malted. And the only female I ever loved enough to want to marry. That makes me crazy.

No one should want to marry a gal like Andrea. She's trouble. She's danger. She's the red signal down the track that says stop! Stop right now, buddy, and take a siding—before the crash.

Trouble will follow Andrea until she's forty, maybe fifty. If someone doesn't strangle her before that. I mean it. Just strangle the life out of her. You can almost feel it in the air around her. It's got to happen. Because out of that man jam, there's always one, just one is all you need, that takes himself and Andrea too seriously. Then snap! His ego breaks like a guitar string wound too tight. And a broken ego has to kick out at someone to make itself feel big again.

You take an ego broken by Andrea and that's the brokenest goddamn ego you're gonna find anywhere. Brother, you can just stop looking.

Anyway, that's what happened to Howie. The string broke and the backlash whipped him down. And he was just a bystander, really. Isn't that always the way? He's just standing on the corner whistling his little tune, and wham! He never knew what hit him, much less why. And all the time the sights should have been swung just a little to the left to pull down the trouble at its source.

Of course, anyone can have good hindsight and secretly I was just as glad to see Howie go as anyone. Maybe a little more so. Nothing very personal. He was just in the light. You couldn't see through him to Andrea. But it seems to me this was only a very temporary measure. You don't stop the hounds by killing one of them. You shoot the fox.

When you come right down to it, Andrea is no better than a two-dollar pro. She's worse. A pro gives to you and takes your money and the transaction is over. With Andrea, it's never over. She clings and clings, draining your blood like a vampire bat, while fanning you with lies to keep you asleep. All she wants is the blood, but she takes your heart along with it.

Well, so what? You can't take it too seriously. The world is full of crazy people who know not what they do or why they do it. And if you happen to fall in love with one of them—that's your hard luck. But you would think that with your eyes open you could keep from walking into a stone wall. Wouldn't you?

Of course, I don't care what a girl is if I happen to love her. She can be a pro, or she can give it to her friends and have no enemies, like Andrea; she can be a waitress, a debutante or a wrestler. It doesn't matter. I don't have much phony pride.

The thing is to live, brother. Just live! Choke the life out of every second in every minute of every hour. Because that goddamn clock is going beep-bop, beep-bop, beep-bop around and around and doesn't care if you're having a ball or bored stiff. And there isn't a beep or a bop you can ever call back, mister. And just remember there are only so many of them—just so many until the last bop.

And if your name is Howard D. Overholtzer or maybe Andrea Lockridge, the clock is a time bomb waiting to go off in your face any second.

We walk around in a dream and we talk about death

in the third person or neuter gender. Death is an IT. And It happened to him—or her. And all the time death is wearing a sly smile because It knows what It is. It is I—first person, singular pronoun—sooner or later.

And death is so inevitable, so objectively known and subjectively unknown that we have to make little jokes about it; jokes about the undertaker and how you can't take it with you and drink up you're dead a long time. That last is the best. You don't mean it when you say it. But you should! You should think about it a long time and then forget it and start laughing like crazy at all the big shots and the little shots who just feel big and the social distinctions, race segregations, sexes, money grabbers, egos and egocentrics. All the egos go into the mill in different sizes and shapes and come out ground to the same fine dust.

You take anyone, man, woman or child and unwind them until the stuffing shows. And what do you think you'll find? Ego! The stuffing, the very core is ego. In the secret places where they live they want to know if they look a little better, say it better, do it better or have it better than the next one. That's all. And that's the truth. And what does it matter? In the end. Just keep on laughing like crazy. Have a ball!

And if something or someone gets in the way of your laughter—think hard and look close. Then if you can get away with it, if it isn't going to boomerang, remove that something or someone in the best way you can. Do it without malice or envy, frustration or regret. Because those are all boomerangs, consuming you, consuming time. Just do it. And go right on laughing and having a ball.

Most of the time I can even laugh at Andrea. Most of the time I won't let myself hate her. And when I do I always come around to seeing how foolish it is. What is Andrea? Or anyone? A thinking mass of matter that got into its present shape by pure accident. Like a half dozen beakers of chemical solutions fell off a shelf to the floor and got all mixed together and this was the end result. Can you blame the beakers? Or the fall? Or the chemicals? Or the final mixture? The final mixture is made up of nothing more than hereditary matter. And mind processed by environment and experience. A tortured environment and a sorry experience equal a mixed up mind. And who's to blame? It's mostly beyond tracing.

And don't give me that old song and dance about, yes, but we can shape experience. The whole thing was rigged. The chemicals were set to react as only those particular chemicals can. Ad nauseum.

I used to tell Andrea, "So you're stacked like one in a million. So what? Don't be so proud, honey. In a few years you'll start coming unstacked. Eventually you'll come unglued right down to the toenails. You better save up a few good jokes and a little dance for that time, honey. You better get ready to play character parts." How we used to laugh at that one after she got through pouting. But what I didn't tell her was that she'll have one hell of a lot bigger party than most until that time comes. If she lives long enough. And maybe her kind should pack up and steal away before the party's over. Because after the music stops, she'll be dead inside anyway.

But I'm just another haphazard mixture of chemicals myself. And I was set to react, to fairly explode, for someone like Andrea. I've stopped fighting it. I'm going to swim right along with it—whatever. What love is when you take it all apart and examine it, I don't know. And don't want to. All I know is that I've got it for her. Or is it vice versa?

I remember the first time we met. I had been out on a date with a noisy blonde. One of those firecrackers that explodes all evening and then fizzles out at the door to her lonely apartment.

She made me restless and on the way home I stopped by a little combination bar and jive joint at the west end of the Strip. For a fast one.

There was a five piece combo and on the doily-sized dance floor, Andrea was dancing with a tall, sissy type who turned out to be Mark Bristol. I never could understand what she saw in him. But then women are beyond logic and I supposed he had some talents that didn't show.

She was decked in one of those low neck jobs with silver sequins. Someone must have died the day it was designed because it was set at about half mast. The long red hair, the beautiful innocence of that face didn't seem to go with the body at all. One argued against the other and I had to settle the argument.

They were playing some Latin thing and I sat on the bar stool, one foot dangling and tapping the floor. Cheek-boom-cheek-boom-cheeka-boom. It made your blood bubble. It made you light enough to fly. It was the sensuous rhythm of life, on the edge of laughter and a dream of floating power. And all the time her high, snooty fanny waved politely—cheek-boom-cheek-boom-cheeka-boom. And I thought, This is it. This is it! No holds barred. What you need, lovely one, is a man. A man! Cheek-boom-cheek-boom-cheeka-boom . . .

I waited until the music stopped and they passed right by me on the way to their table. Then I said, "Well, hello there!" Just as if we were old soulmates. She knew I was talking to her because she could certainly see where I was looking.

She stopped on his arm and turned toward me. For a moment her face was perfectly blank and I thought I had made the wrong play and fumbled the ball. I should have sneaked around left end.

But then her lips, those twenty-carat rubies for which I later hocked my soul, twisted slowly upwards in a rather bewildered but pleased expression. "Don't tell me," she said. "It's coming up slowly out of deep water." Then she snapped her fingers. "Got it! You're Bud . . . Bud Masterson, class of fifty-one, U.C.L.A., All-American. Half back, wasn't it?"

"Right!" I said. And waited.

"And I'm Andrea Lockridge, class of fifty-two, and how are you? It's been a long time."

"Hasn't it," I said. "Just wanted to say hello." Of course, I had never met her in my life and she knew it. U.C.L.A. is a big place. But thank God for a little fame and a face just ugly enough to remember.

She introduced me to Mark then, he of the slight scowl and the on-the-mark, ready, let's run stance. I gave him the big, cordial smile and she said, "Will you have a drink with us?"

"No thanks," I said. "I don't like to make a crowd of myself. But I'll beg a dance next set if that's all right?"

She was quite willing and when I took her from Mark, I wanted to give him my handkerchief because I thought he was going to cry.

We danced not one dance, but a whole set. I fell in love with her the first moment we touched and never got over it. But I didn't let on that I knew we had never met. You can't pull down their tattered flag of moral pretense.

Still, the knowledge made me brave enough to say, "You're too marvelous not to share yourself. I wish you had a late date list and I was on it. Tonight!"

Her laughter was like a conspiracy. "You know," she said. "I'm suddenly developing a splitting headache." And then she whispered, "Call me in an hour. We'll arrange something." She gave me her number.

I work hard to make all my hours short with excitement. But that was the longest hour I ever remember.

Eventually I found myself at her apartment. About two o'clock in the morning. She had on that same gown when she came to the door. Her breasts made a long white dip before, with saucy irritation at confinement, they pulled up sharp beneath the dress. Her lips were parted in the same conspiratorial smile she gave me on the dance floor. Already I could feel the long taper of her body against me, the sensual nudge of perfume from her hair, a vague promise, subtle as a sigh.

I've never felt the slightest inclination to force myself on any female. But, at that moment, the flush of

longing was so overpowering that she seemed the
composite of all the women who had ever teased and
run to hide behind the protection of the weaker sex.
I felt ten feet tall. The muscles of my biceps flexed,
my legs tightened. And I thought, this one's not going
to get away. I could hold her so easily in one arm and
slowly rip her clothes away, glad to pay the price.

"Hello . . ." she said. "Hello!"

I stepped through the doorway and she closed the
door behind me. "Where would you like to go?" I said
in a hoarse whisper.

"Go?" she said. "You're here. Isn't that enough?"

We had a drink. And we danced to the radio. There
was only one light. It came from the kitchen. "It's
better," she said. "I wouldn't want anyone to drive by
and think I was home."

"There must be a hundred men who would drive by
checking," I said as we danced.

Her body settled against me and reached a point of
agreement with mine. "There would be a thousand,"
she said. "If there were that many who really knew
me."

"Aren't you a little afraid, being alone with me?"

"Not yet," she said. "Make me afraid."

Then I kissed her and went suddenly numb and
brainless.

"Now the only thing I'm afraid of is that you'll stop,"
she murmured.

That was when I almost tore that dress from her
body. I would have, too. Except that her fingers raced
to help me.

I knew almost from the beginning what she was and
how she was. And I didn't care. I cared only that it
wouldn't stop. Ever. I was grateful to be accepted as
even one of many. For awhile. And then I wanted to
erase the others like so many obscene drawings on a
blackboard.

She got a permanent grip on me in the only way she
could. By adding affection and kindness, a mother's

gentleness, to passion. And a big dose of humor. We were always laughing. Like crazy. She had the most instinctive knowledge of the many facets of a man's need. And in the end, used that knowledge to entangle me and then betray me.

The time came when I asked her to marry me. I didn't think she would. I was sure she wasn't the type. But surprisingly she said yes, she thought it was a wonderful idea but she needed time. She wanted to be fair to us both and not rush into it. Would I wait a couple of months or so and give her free rein while she got used to the idea of dedicating herself to one man? I had no choice. I said yes, I would wait but did she really love me? Yes, she really, really loved me.

I waited.

I knew money was no small issue with her. She always talked obliquely of living on a grand scale. I didn't have too much money. Not the kind she was dreaming of. I had gone into partnership with a man who wanted to open a couple of sporting goods stores. He put up most of the money and I lent my name to the business. It was a pretty big name then. He ran one store and I ran the other. We sold everything from guns to tennis rackets. And did a nice business. When Andrea came along I could see the handwriting on the marriage certificate so I persuaded my partner to open still another store—in Santa Monica. That store failed pretty badly and dragged down the take supporting it.

Then along came Howie Overholtzer and I got the brush—a nice, warm, friendly brush that didn't want to sweep me clean but keep me still dangling. I wasn't taken in by that. I knew it was over.

The trouble was that it was too late in the game for it to be over for me. I had been swimming downstream with her over a lot of rapids and I was in deep. I couldn't reverse myself. I tried laughing on the inside, the way I do when things bust for me. I used to sit with my ear glued to my mind and listen for that laughter. I listened a long time. But I never heard so much as a chuckle.

Well, like I said awhile back—if something or someone gets in the way of your laughter, think hard and look close. Then if you can get away with it, if it isn't going to boomerang, remove that something or someone in the best way you can and go right on laughing and having a ball.

I looked very hard and I looked very close. And while I was looking, Howie Overholtzer got shot in all the right places.

And now I'm laughing again. Like crazy.

Andrea Lockridge

IT'S SUNDAY AGAIN. This was the day I was to have been married. It's so sad. I feel awful. Just awful! Poor Howie. And poor Andrea!

Bud Masterson was over last night. He was quite gay and I got to giggling in spite of everything. But then we found that humor and love-making don't mix. So we got very serious.

Bud is another rope around my neck that I'm going to have to untie pretty quickly in order to marry Doug. I haven't told Doug yet. But I'm going to when he comes over tonight.

And now I've seen them all—Doug, Jeff, Mark, Ralph and Bud. The men in my life. I love them all— each in a different way. I hate to part with any one of them but I suppose I'm going to have to since there are bound to be hard feelings.

Hard feelings! It could be worse than that. Anything could happen. What am I going to do? What-shall-I-do! Disappear. That's it. Just disappear with Doug. Never come back. But what about his work? We have to live. Oh, I don't know. I don't know! I'm so mixed up. And I'm so scared I wish I was locked in a vault.

It seems like forever since last Saturday night when . . . when it happened, Howie already buried and forgotten by most. I didn't even go to the funeral. At the last minute I was too frightened to go out. Poor, lost Howie. I could cry.

Except for Sunday and Monday when Viv and I were alone and I was in such shock, I've been with a different one of my men every night. I suppose in a way it was an absolutely horrible thing to do, practi- cally over Howie's grave. But, after all, we weren't yet married. And I was afraid not to see them. Yes, afraid. That was it. Perfectly excusable and quite understandable. I won't think about it another minute. We do what we have to do as bravely as we can. Life must go on.

I had the most wonderful talk with Ralph when he was here Friday night. Ralph is quite religious and so am I. We got to talking about God and about death and about the life hereafter.

"Do you think there is any hope that we have some kind of life after death?" I asked him.

"Yes," he said. "I think there is at least a strong hope, though I don't think we go to a place called heaven or hell, anything like that. I think we enter a new state of mind and make our own heaven or hell as we do here."

"That sounds terribly involved," I said. "Then what is death, really?"

He smiled, a little sadly. "That's one question that makes a joke of all the others. Not even Jesus gave us a clear answer. But I think that death is another phase of the dream called life. It's really an awakening.

"Did you ever have a dream something like this? You're on the edge of a cliff. You see a solid mass of rock far below. Suddenly you are pushed (Howard was pushed) or you stumble (like those who die without violence) and you fall. Down and down you go, the rock rushing to meet you. And as you fall, it is the moment of the utmost fear, like the instant you know that death is swallowing you. And then—and then, at the moment of impact, even as you feel a dart of pain, you wake up! And you look around you and you're home. Home! The sun shining through your window, the familiar sounds just outside, the known bed with its covers touched by your fingers.

"And this is the end of fear and the beginning of a boundless joy. You are not dead. You were never even touched. Not a hair of your head. It was just a dream. So then, death is an instant of fear, the culmination of fear, the greatest fear of your life. A pulse beat in time. And then you wake up.

"But did you ever have a dream like that?"

"Not with the cliff," I said. "But very much like it. The result was the same. Oh, Ralph. Ralph! What a marvelous thing you've said. If only it were true. What proof, what proof in the world do we have of eternity?"

"None. But our own knowing. It seems clear to me that if man can conceive of eternity, it exists. Man would not be able to imagine eternity if it did not exist. All things of which man has conceived have come true or are yet to come. Jesus did promise eternal life. And in Psalms it says, 'A thousand years are but a watch in the night to the Lord.'"

"Ralph, I want to cry. I just want to cry. But that part about the cliff. Is that what happened to Howie? Did he just fall almost to the bottom and then wake up? Is that what happened to Howie?"

"Yes," he said. "That's what happened to Howie." He spoke as though to a little girl and with the tender smile you give a little girl who wants to believe the marvelous fable. And yet as I looked into his eyes, I was sure that he meant every word of it.

"Ralph," I said, "I wish that I could . . . I mean, there's just no one like you in the whole world. What's wrong with me, Ralph? What is wrong with me!"

"Nothing," he said. "Except that you need love. Not the kind you've been getting in some places, but real love. Selfless understanding. We all need that love, Andrea. Every one of us, no matter how smug and closed within, needs pure love. And because we didn't get it when we needed it most, we changed and changed and changed. We built our walls of selfishness and sharpened our defenses."

"Do you have that pure love for me, Ralph?"

"One big part of me has that pure love and the other part is shamefully selfish and base. I wish it wasn't so. In a way."

I felt so terribly close to him at that moment. You

just have no idea. "Ralph," I said. "I want to ask you something I've been afraid to ask anyone else. Do you think that a man like Willie Switzer or some complete stranger killed Howie? Or . . . or do you think he was killed by . . . by one of the other men I call my lovers? Is it possible?"

He looked at me steadily for a long moment. The moment grew and grew until I wanted to scream, until I began to doubt him, even him, and wanted to run from the sight of his eyes. But finally he said, "Yes, it's possible that it was one of your lovers, Andrea. In fact, I've been quite sure of it from the beginning. Because this was an intensely personal killing, conceived by a mind more diabolically clever and imaginative, containing a deeper vessel for love and cancerous hate than any of the Willie Switzers of the world . . .

"Oh, now, Andrea darling. I'm sorry. Don't cry. Don't cry, baby. Here, let me hold you. I didn't mean to scare you. I only said it for your own protection. Let me hold you, dear."

"Don't touch me," I said. "Don't touch me!" I shouted. And I was scared. I was scared like that falling over the cliff. I was scared like that awful moment as you shatter against the rocks below. Because I didn't think I was ever going to wake up.

I didn't think I would ever leave my apartment alive.

The Murderer

IT ALL WORKED OUT so beautifully. Even better than I had hoped. It was neat as a problem in geometry with all the angles figured, all the lines coming together and meeting where they should. And the first, simple rule was the best: The shortest distance between the gun barrel and Howard Overholtzer was a straight line. Also, a bullet for Howie was the shortest distance between me and Andrea Lockridge.

But mathematics is a cold and bloodless science. It doesn't figure on the human element, which is full of changing factors, unpredictable emotions. This, being human also, is where I slipped. I didn't figure that Andrea, being a woman of the type blown by the wind of every emotion and seldom steadied by logic, would be just the sort who would signal a right turn and then go left.

It isn't a turn that she has made, but one that she is going to make. I can see it coming. And since I will be standing right in her path, I'll be run down and squashed like some rodent too small and nasty even to be noticed. If it didn't happen this time, it would happen sooner or later. I can see that—now. Too late. Too late!

So this is the end of the matter. For her and for me. And I want everyone to share it. I want everyone to be in on the glorious, glorious finish. I want to be there myself at the end of her reign, applauding her exit. And I will. Because wherever I'm going, she will precede me.

But in the beginning, it all worked out so beautifully. Even now, no one suspects. Idiots! They don't have the vaguest idea of who did it, much less why. They think the motive was jealousy. Or just plain lust. Of course, in a way, they're right. Because it was a combination of both. But a different kind of jealousy and a different kind of lust than they would understand or could ever know.

But as to the simple problem of whodunit, who murdered the bastard, they're sniffing around the wrong tree and they're lost in a forest of probabilities. They make me laugh and I want to take them by their sweaty hands and say, Here, fellas, here, boys, sniff over this way. What about me? Do you think anyone else is so capable and so cool, so without silly conscience and tearful remorse?

I don't think they'll ever find the rifle, the beautiful, beautiful rifle, so precise, so unemotionally obedient, but now rusting at the bottom of the ocean. Yet still within reach of the most idiot skin diver. And even if they do find it by some blundering accident, I don't think there's a chance in the world they could trace it to me.

I loved that rifle. Because I loved its owner. It belonged to my brother. I had an unusually strong affection for him. He understood me in a way that no one has before or since. I hated my father and especially my mother, both of whom, seated blissfully in the dining car, died stupidly in a stupid train wreck, their dumb mouths undoubtedly open with surprise, like imbecile fish speared in the most profound act of their lives—gorging themselves with food.

But I loved my brother, my older brother, who took over the job my parents had mangled, a little too late. I worshipped him. In a sense, he made me what I wanted to be and never before could come close to being—a man! He taught me to ride and swim and hunt, and while still a kid, to think with the hard, clear knowing of a man.

And then one day on a deer hunt, the woods swarming with mindless apes behind guns, we stood for a moment watching a deer bounding out of range and began to follow.

I never heard the shot; or, I heard too many shots to tell one from another. But suddenly my brother paused in stride and shivered the way an animal does to shake off a fly. He turned to me with a look of utter calm and said quietly, "Here—take my gun. I've been hit." And then with a bullet through his chest, he just nodded off to sleep and sank to the ground.

It was like a movie scene you can't bear and with sheer will you try to force into reverse. Take it back. Take it back! Make the bullet fly backward into the unknown barrel it came from. Make my brother rise slowly the way he fell, and smiling, stride forward again.

But it wasn't a movie and the scene had reeled and wouldn't unreel. Ever.

Right then, something was taken from me. The last love I had for any person or thing on earth. Until I met Andrea. And worshipped her like my brother. I mean only in degree, not at all in kind.

And now I have stopped worshipping Andrea. I hate her! Far from saving her, I would like to complete her debasement. In fact, it comes to me now that I must never have loved or worshipped her at all, that I despised all she represented and merely wanted to endear myself to her long enough to pull down her lofty tower with my own secret debasement.

But as to the rifle, it was about all that my brother left me. So I loved it. I practiced with it until I could have won almost any contest in marksmanship. And then one day I put it away as merely a keepsake hidden in the bottom of an old trunk, keeping it secret for some reason I don't understand; unless I was waiting for an excuse to revenge the loss of my brother by riding the world of an ass like Overholtzer who had no right to breathe air while my brother, a god of a man, was already eight years dead.

Anyway, Overholtzer was a simple shot for me. I knew it might have to happen just that way, so I went off to a deserted spot and practiced until I was almost as good as I used to be. Periodically, I had cleaned and oiled the gun with something like affection and it was in fine shape. When I had to drop it in the ocean, it was as much like losing the last evidence of my brother as losing the evidence of a crime.

One thing I remember thinking just before I pulled the trigger. I thought, You may be a queen, honey bitch, but I'm a god. And I'm going to use my power to take from you what you want most in the world.

It all went so nicely after that, so sweetly. I was so sympathetic. And like I knew she would, she cried on my shoulder, while the hand that had killed her lover, her bag of gold, caressed her and helped her undress. And then later, I lay next to her big body in the warm bed and gave her the strange, forbidden comfort she needed. It seemed a long time since she had allowed me to touch her and I took advantage of her phony sorrow and real fear to drag her down—even below the level of her own cesspool.

And the goddamnedest thing about it was that the big bitch never lost her erotic tendencies even for a day! She was ready like Peter Rabbit even before the sound of the shot died away. What a laugh that gave me. And it was a real bonus because I had expected to wait a week or more to even get near her.

But now she smiles in all the right places and inwardly turns against me. Even her body, that lovely but accidental assembly, will shrink from me now, as it will the others. I don't hear what she says because I know her. She has plans. She always has plans. But don't count on them, little girl. Don't count on them.

This is Sunday and the bridegroom cometh not. For he is shot. And I don't mean half shot, brother!

But yesterday afternoon I did a little shopping in one of our better department stores. I had to buy some shoes. Then I got to browsing around with nothing particular in mind. And while I was in the basement looking for some bargain on anything at all, I came across a better bargain than I ever imagined. It was for free!

I was drifting past that array of stuff called household utensils. And then I spied it shining smack in the center of all that cutlery. And something terribly clever and full of grotesque humor popped into my fertile brain.

But what caught my attention was this: It was a cleaver. A meat cleaver. Not one of those lusterless and awkward looking things you see rusting around a butcher shop, either. A nice, refined one for home use. It was somewhat smaller and slightly curved with an ebony handle. It was strong looking and made of stainless steel, as neat and shining as a surgical instrument. It was a little beauty fit for a queen!

I picked it up by the handle. It was heavy but perfectly balanced and compact. I put it down again and, staring at it, began to think of Andrea's wedding and how disappointed she must be. Then I thought of how it would be nice to hold a wedding party anyway, and somehow get all her lovers to attend. Only this would be a wedding party in reverse—if you see what I mean.

I checked around carefully and when no one was looking, I snatched up the cleaver and stuck it under my jacket, finally working it around so that it was under my arm and I could hold it against my side and not drop it.

While I was sauntering out of the store as nonchalantly as could be, I got to juggling a funny old rhyme until it came out just right. And then it got to going round and round in my head and wouldn't stop. I heard it over and over again—All the queen's horses and all the queen's men . . . All the queen's horses and all the queen's men . . .

I almost laughed out loud.

Douglas Coleman

I DIDN'T SLEEP WELL last night. As usual I'm troubled about Andrea. But this is special. There is something in the wind that makes me uneasy. I have the feeling that the Overholtzer killing was wasted on Andrea, that you could kill them all and she'd still find another mess to get into.

But last night (Saturday night) I was so restless I could hardly stay in bed. I knew Bud Masterson was up there because I called Vivian Manbee at her office and she told me. I had that same wretched impulse to go up there and stand watching in the dark until he came out.

But finally I fought it down and went to sleep for a short time, coming wide awake suddenly, jumping out of bed and starting to put my clothes on before I knew why, then going back to bed and finally to sleep again. I seem to be in an advanced state of shock all the time.

However, in the process of waking up suddenly like that, I crystalized something about sleep I have been searching for a long time. We never enjoy the so-called comfort of black or dreamless sleep. We only think we don't dream. What actually happens is that we don't remember. That is, we remember some dreams but not others. The memory of some dreams vanishes the instant we wake up.

I found a way to prove it. Before I went to sleep, I would tell myself to concentrate on remembering the second I woke up. I did, and discovered that I could grab the tail end of a dream memory and pull it right up into consciousness every time. Then I could rebuild the dream, put it together fragment by fragment. The experiment only convinced me that we are mentally

130

active every moment, awake or asleep. This could lead to other conclusions—about death—that are stranger still. Why am I always thinking about death?

Viv gave me a rundown of what's been going on, Andrea seeing all her boys, and apparently making new promises of marriage and eternal bliss to each of them, and only meaning it with Jeff, so that I can now discount anything Andrea has said or will say to me. And Viv, changing tack now, advises that I forget Andrea completely, just not see her at all since she is hopeless and will only manage to ". . . destroy someone as deep and sincere as you are, Doug." But I told her I have traveled much too far not to go all the way now, if for no other reason than mere curiosity. It's like hating the ordeal of life but not firing a bullet through your brain because you want to know how the whole gloomy story turns out.

I talked to Andrea herself yesterday and it seems that my turn on her roster comes up again tonight. Viv is going out around eight and I am due at nine. Andrea hints that she has something vital to tell me concerning us. She was so superbly sweet and affectionate with me on the phone that I can just imagine what's coming. This is the prelude to a final brush off. She probably is going to marry Jeff, since he is now at the top of the list as Mr. Moneyman. Well, I don't want to hear it. I won't listen.

She'll never get the words out of her mouth.

Vivian Manbee

IT'S TWENTY-FIVE MINUTES PAST SEVEN, Sunday night with Andrea still unmarried, although this was to be her wedding day. Andrea and I have just had a nasty fight and I'm going out earlier than I expected. I don't know where I'm going and I don't care. Just out. Out!

Andrea just now hinted that I have overstayed my welcome and that I am in the way of her amours. Imagine! After all I've done for her and after I have practically walked the streets night after night so she can carry on her messy writhings with her messy men.

For the first time, I openly lost my temper and asked her if she didn't need me as a kind of pimp to drum up business. I can think of a dozen answers she could have cut me down with, but she resorted to her usual display of shock, followed by tears, the defense of all cloying females with more bust than brain. I just walked out of the room and left her sobbing on the bed.

This is the end of the line for me. In a way, I'm glad. I could puke over the whole deal. I don't know what's going to happen to me now and I don't give much of a goddamn. But on my way out there are a few little things I want to attend to for Andrea.

I think it's time I straightened out a few people. So I'm going down now and place a few calls. I'm going to call each one of Andrea's deceived and tell him, oh, so confidentially, that Andrea is now going to marry Doug Coleman, and that as Andrea hints, they are just going to slip away—just disappear. Of course, I have already left Doug in a state of uncertainty, insinuating that Andrea is about to take the next biggest hunk of gold —Jeff Slater.

But can you imagine the stir this little gem of news will cause? "It's just for your own good, Jeff (or Mark, or Ralph, or Bud) that I want to tell you what Andrea is about to do to you. After all, you're too deep and sincere to be destroyed by this kind of evil that Andrea represents and I want to protect you from further hurt."

Can you imagine what malevolent ideas will come to them? Not half so malevolent, however, as my own final hatred for her.

Anyway, I'm going to make those calls. I'm going to bring the snake out of hiding and give each one a club. But while the clubs are being raised, it will appear that I am far removed from the scene. So now I will give Andrea what she wants.

I'm going out right now and leave her.

Alone.

Andrea Lockridge

IT'S FIVE MINUTES TO EIGHT and Doug is due around nine. Viv left about a half hour ago. We had a bad fight, as I knew we would. I cried and she went huffing off somewhere. She practically called me a prostitute. It's the first time in all these years she has really turned on me. Just because I told her that I was getting along fine now and wouldn't she be happier back at her place where she wouldn't have to play nursemaid to me.

There are so many reasons why I can't have Viv around. She seems to stand over me like a silent accusation, a reminder that I am weak and I should reform my moral character. She resents my popularity and my looks more than she ever dares show. She is such a strange little bag of bones that I don't think I have really ever understood her. About two-thirds of her smoulders beneath the surface. And instead of building me up, she drags me down in the most awful way.

I just took a bath and instead of getting dressed as I should, came right back here to lie on the bed in the altogether. Altogether skin. Honestly, I feel so depressed I can hardly breathe. Maybe I am as bad as Viv says I am. This is one of the few times I have ever looked at the truth. Usually I keep it way back in a corner of my mind where it can't touch me.

I just wish they would leave me alone. That's an expression I've been using a lot lately—They. They doesn't mean people necessarily. I guess it means life collectively—the forces that are always hammering against you, that don't let you have what you want, that interfere every turn you make. I just wish *they*

would leave me alone. Life is so uphill discouraging,
it's hardly worth it. You'd think for the short space of
sixty or seventy years *they* would just leave you alone
and let you have fun. Life is a loan and *they* collect
soon enough. Sometimes, like Howie, They collect
before the note is due.

Anyway, you don't think much about your faults
until someone gets mad and gives you a close-up
look at yourself, however unfair or exaggerated. I
would prefer not to think too much but just go on
feeling my way through life and kind of living on
instinct. Thinking makes you sad that you can't
do better—or just won't. But I'm going to try. I'll try
tomorrow. Monday is always a good day to start a
diet or some kind of reform. I'll try tomorrow.

The police have now questioned and investigated
all my men and don't seem to be getting anywhere.
I talked to Lieutenant Brehmer yesterday and he said
that none of my friends have any police record whatsoever and that while this doesn't necessarily prove
anything, most murders are committed by people who
at least have a tendency toward violence which shows
up on a police blotter somewhere. Also, almost everyone has a pretty good alibi. For instance, Doug was
with Viv and she backs him up. Mark was with his
roommate who saw him asleep at three A.M., Ralph
was with his mother in Laguna and Bud was at a
party that lasted most of the night, although it was
a pretty drunken affair and he might have slipped out.
Jeff claims he was asleep by eleven, though, he can't
prove it and they had a man tailing him for awhile
but got nothing on him. So it still narrows down
to Willie Switzer and the hunt is on for him in a big
way.

But I keep remembering Ralph's eyes when I asked
him if he thought one of my lovers did it. For a minute
I thought that he had some secret knowledge because
he was so shockingly positive—or that maybe he . . .
But heavens, I was just scared and when he left I
was absolutely convinced that that sweet, compas-

sionate man is incapable of hurting another human being. But he is so terribly deep and perceiving that I know he's right. One of those men who took my love and my body killed Howie Overholtzer.

God in heaven! Can I lie here all alone and even think such a thing? I won't think about it at all. I just won't!

Well, now it's all over and I'm going to be able to breathe again. This chronic fear that trembles inside me will be cured like some filthy growth just cut right out or dissolved in happiness and freedom. Because when Doug comes, I'm going to tell him I never really loved or wanted anyone else. Then we will sneak off tomorrow or maybe tonight and I'll never come back to this place. I'll have Viv or someone send me what things I can't take and sublet my apartment for the rest of the lease. The only piece of furniture I own is that vanity with the big mirror I take everywhere.

Doug and I will be married, probably in Vegas, and then I'll have the first security of my life. I don't think I'll ever see any of the others again because I'll always be wondering if . . . There I go again! I mustn't think about it.

It's so quiet and so lonely! I hope Doug isn't late. My God! What time is it? Ten after eight. Well . . . Another ten minutes and I'll start getting dressed.

Maybe I should just lie here naked for Doug. No, I'd have to go let him in. Did I put the chain on the door? No, because I wasn't even in the room when Viv left. Well . . .

I do have a nice body. Even I can see that. Even lying on my back my breasts don't sag. And my tummy is almost flat. Oh, dear! Remember the time I thought I was pregnant? But it was a false alarm and I'm always so careful. You just have to be because you . . .

What was that? What *was* that! I'm sure I heard the door opening . . . Yes! Now it's closing. So quietly and . . .

I hear someone coming, walking so . . . Walking

so softly! My God, my God! Viv won't be back for hours and so who? . . . Did I give anyone a key? I can't think. Can't think! Or did Viv leave the door open when she went off so angry and . . .

Where can I hide! Where can I hide? Too late now, he's . . . he's almost . . . Dear God! My Father. Save me like you did before. Save me—save me!

I've got to say something. Anything! Can't speak. Can't . . .

"Hello! Is someone there? Who is it please? Don't come in, I . . . I'm not dressed. Is that you, Doug? Doug!"

Get to the phone! Quick! No. Oh, God. It's in the other room! My heart is beating so and I can't breathe and I . . .

"Listen! Whoever you are out there, I'm going to call the police if you don't answer me . . . Answer me! Answer me!

"Answer meee!"

The Murderer

I LOOKED AROUND CAREFULLY outside her door. There
was no one in sight. I didn't much care anyway because even if I got caught, it didn't matter now. But
there were reasons why I was quite sure they wouldn't
suspect me.

I opened the door and went in quietly, closing and
locking it with the chain. Even if she screamed—and
I didn't think she would—it would be too late.

I didn't have to be quiet. I could have calmed her
just by calling out. But the fear is the best part of
it and I could tell by her voice that she was shaking
to pieces with terror and I wanted to prolong it. Finally
I opened the bedroom door. Very slowly.

She was lying nude on the bed, her arms stretched
apart, her hands grasping the sides of the mattress.
Her eyes were wide with shock, her big, red mouth
gaping, her great milky breasts heaving. She saw me.

"It's you!" she said. "My God. Oh, my God! I was
so scared. So scared!" She exhaled and sank back
from her stupid straining, closing her eyes and swallowing so that her Adam's apple jerked back and forth.
Oh, it was wonderful. Wonderful!

"Why didn't you speak?" she said. "Why didn't you
say something?"

I smiled. I didn't answer. She kept searching my
face, still frightened but calming down.

"Why do you look at me so strangely?" she said.
"And what are you doing here anyway? You know
that I . . ."

"I wanted to talk to you," I said. My voice was
husky with conflicting needs. She was so startlingly
naked and beautiful on the bed.

"What did you want to talk to me about? Is . . . is there something wrong? I have to get dressed. And what have you got there, for heaven's sake? In the package."

"It's a little present for you," I said.

"Oh! How nice. How sweet!"

I laid the package on her dressing table. It made a small thud. She didn't notice.

"Aren't you going to give it to me?"

"Oh, yes!" I said. "In a minute. Be patient, sweetie."

I stood over her for a moment. Then I leaned down and ran my hand slowly over her body.

"Don't," she said, shrinking back a little from me.

"You used to like it," I said. "Only last week, you . . ."

"That's finished," she said. "I was upset and didn't know what I was doing."

I went on caressing her. "There was a time before that when you were quite willing. Remember?"

"I don't want to remember," she said. "It was a long time ago and I didn't know how evil it was. I was really a child and you appealed to my emotions. That side of me is dead. Forever. I loathe it."

"It wasn't dead last week, baby," I stroked her.

"Don't! Take your hands off me, you filthy thing. You disgust me! You're just like a dirty, crawling spider waiting for a victim. Ugh! You look like a spider, too. Get out! Get out of here. And don't come back!"

I wanted that. I needed her to say that. Maybe if she hadn't . . . But she did. I took my hand away from her and walked over to the dresser. I picked up the package. It was heavy. "Want your present, honey?"

"No! I don't want your dirty present. Or you! Just please get out."

"Such gratitude," I said. "Such sweet gratitude. Well, I'll unwrap it for you."

I unwound the cotton string and the flimsy paper with which I had wrapped it, dropping it to the floor.

I got a firm grip on the ebony handle. Her head was turned away from me. I walked to her side. She turned and saw.

"What have you got there?" she said. Her eyes began to dilate slightly. She still wasn't certain.

"This is my present," I said. "Isn't it a beauty? Fit for a queen!"

"What . . . what is it? Is . . . is that a knife or—"

"It's a guillotine," I said.

"A what?" She swallowed and I was fascinated by her Adam's apple.

"A guillotine," I said again. "The reign of the queen is over and I have commanded that she shall be executed in the manner of all queens." It struck me funny and I could feel the laughter bubbling inside of me, not sure if I really laughed out loud.

"What . . . what are you . . . you talking about?" she stuttered. "You're crazy!" she knew then. She knew about Howie, too, but she couldn't say it. Her hands were gripping the mattress again and her eyes were enormous. They bulged from her head. I wanted her to look just like that for her lovers—afterwards.

"Please," she said. "Please! Calm down. Don't you know that I love you, that I always have. Here. Come, dear. Come lie by my side and we'll talk it all over."

I raised the little guillotine, with its surgical gleam, a little higher. Her face was as white as her breasts. She kept wetting her dry lips.

"What . . . what are you going to do with that?" she whispered.

"I'm going to cut off your head," I said quietly.

"What?"

"I'm going to cut off your head and put it on the dining-room table for everyone to see. And then I'm going to prop your body up in a chair right next to it. Can you picture it? Can't you see it!"

I grabbed her hair and pulled her head back. Her white neck was perfectly exposed. I raised the cleaver.

"Vivian!" She screamed. "Don't do it. I love you! I love you! Vivian! Oh, God save me. Viv—ian!"

There was a terrible crash. A big fist pushed through the blind and the glass of the window, shattering it over the floor.

But it was too late. I brought the cleaver down with all my might. Chop! It went right on through the bed. It was stuck in the mattress and I couldn't get it out.

Then I looked down.

She was gone. She was standing naked by the man who had come through the window. He was holding her up. The man was Willie Switzer. When I had looked toward the sound of the crash, she had slipped out of my grasp to the floor and crawled to him.

Now he dropped her and came toward me. I pulled on the handle, but the cleaver was sunk into the bedding. He put his big, hairy arm under my chin and against my neck. He pulled back and we both fell to the floor. It was over.

Doug Coleman was the first to come. Even before the police.

Andrea sat slumped in a chair, sobbing. She had on a bathrobe. Doug stood over her, stroking her head and looking from me to Switzer and back again. Switzer stood guard over my chair, his long, dirty hair half over his eyes.

"Coupla goddamn lesbians," he said. "I seen 'em through the window. I seen 'em before, too—last Monday night. Only this time, Andrea, she didn't want no part of this one. So this one here tried to chop her head off with a meat axe. Goddamndest thing I ever seen. I come in through that there window just in time."

Doug didn't answer. He just looked at Andrea with this sad, sad expression. I know he was going to forgive her. Even that he was going to forgive her.

I heard the sirens then. Like I heard them the night on the pier. First one and then another. And then another. Only this time, there was no satisfaction. And no place to hide.

The others were outside watching when they took me down the steps, Jeff, Mark, Bud and Ralph. I had told each one that Andrea would be alone at nine o'clock if they wanted to see her. And she would have been alone, too. She would have been alone—naked and waiting—on the table and in the chair.

But now I am alone—waiting for the loneliest time of all. Yet, I'm not afraid. Because I ask you? In the life beyond, if there is one, in the dark void of nothingness, in death itself—

Could there be a deeper loneliness than has followed me all my life?

The End